Lively Hope
BOOKS & MORE

ISBN 979-8-9872509-3-8

Cover and interior design by Rich Carnahan, Publish Pros

ARLENA RETURNS

THE SEQUEL TO *CHARLESTON'S ELEGANT SINNERS*

TERRY WARD TUCKER

What would happen if one woman told the truth about her life? The world would split open.

Muriel Rukeyser

1

I did not fall in love with Hal those first days. I trained myself to look away. He belonged to my friend, Rennie, a circumstance that made him off limits to me. Truth? Hal was too young for either of us…too good-looking, distant, aimless, seductive, the sum of which rendered him irresistible to a free spirit like Rennie, who for a time was giving her wedding band a rest in its original Tiffany's box. I had no inconvenient husband lurking in the background just then, a fact that did not make me younger. It made me divorced. But we were talking about Hal, weren't we? Yes, about Hal. We were talking about him.

As time dragged by after the shooting – I killed my ex-husband's wife, you see, when she tried to steal my children – I discovered a certain sensitivity in Hal hiding beneath the surface, an unexpected warmth that on difficult days had the capacity to melt my frozen heart…around its icy edges at least. Though I still did not fall in love with him. That complication came later over the weeks it took him, along with Rennie, to show me in the context of the unspeakable what real love was all about. Forsake me, they did not. Love me, they did.

2

It rained the night I shot and killed Giselle, Stuart's new wife. I saw the first bright drops as they splashed against the long windows of their darkened living room. I had just realized she was there, just turned to look...when heavier drops began ticking on the gutters outside. Stuart and I did not know she was about. We'd been arguing when she had slipped into the room. Not until she spoke, did we know.

"You can't win, Arlena," she said, the arrogance in her tone revealing she had not seen the revolver in my hands. "Stuart and I have enough on you to take the twins for good. You'll be lucky to get visitation."

It was then I heard the gunshot and felt the quiver of small muscles in my fingers that let me know I had pulled the trigger. Stuart shouted Giselle's name and ran to help her. I observed his panic and wondered at the devastation I had wrought. A river of rain could not wash away my guilt.

I wanted to call the authorities straightaway to confess, but Rennie and Hal said no. For weeks they droned one mantra into my ear: Arlena, you must not take the coward's way out. You must think of Raven and Constantia.

After the shot, I dropped the gun and kicked it under a chair. Even in my confusion, I understood it was an evil thing meant to do evil deeds. I wanted it out of my sight, to undo what it had done, what I had done.

Stuart sank to his knees and bent over Giselle, silent Giselle, Giselle who had not moved since she'd collapsed. I watched him elevate her head and shoulders, try to wake her, get her to speak, breathe. He felt her neck and wrists, pressed an ear to her chest, not that he could have heard heart sounds above the torrent of rain now pelting the glass doors.

He lifted her upper body closer to his. Then he looked back at me. "What have you done?" he said. "What have we done? We can't fix this."

3

Over the long months of my pregnancy, I awoke each morning to the rush and drag of ocean waves. How lovely to rise in that purple hour before dawn and walk the beach in cool half-light. The Atlantic Ocean, alien and shimmering, did not know me, did not welcome me, yet I remained the faithful visitor. In anticipation of daybreak, I would pause at the edge of the surf to contemplate the miracle of saline fluids within and without my body. For a charmed half-hour I'd consider the small twins tumbling about like baby seahorses at play in the waters of my womb.

I felt on these sojourns as if I had been painted into a nighttime seascape, oily blues and blacks applied with slim pallet knife to moonlit ocean and sky, slashes of silver still shiny with brush strokes lighting a wide beach, a figure in a long white robe suspended in the lower left corner, disregarded, as ill of fit as an afterthought.

One morning at first light, a vision of a live silkie, a human child transformed by Gaelic magic into the shape of a seal pup, appeared before me as real or unreal as some blue-misted dream. For I was never certain if the creature I saw diving in and out of the waves was a true seal-child who at any moment might change back into a boy or girl, or only a playful moonbeam bouncing about in the pale of a new dawn.

I loved those mornings. They were treasure gifts from my old friend, Grayson Pinckney, for it was he who insisted I stop working in his office and retire full time to Sullivan's Island to await the birth of my babies. If not for his wisdom, I'd have succumbed to exhaustion every night and slept through weeks of enchanted dawns and Gaelic visitations. I would never have known that my natural rhythm of sleeping and waking was in perfect tune with nature. Until Mr. Pinckney's gift of time, I had believed grim fatigue my normal state. On looking back, I realize that discovering otherwise saved my life in the end. Had I failed to understand over those few lunar cycles my capacity for the unhurried and unharried, I would never have been able four years later to fight my way back from hell.

Mr. Pinckney…you gave me those mornings. Thank you, not for myself, but for my children, Raven and Constantia. You, along with Rennie and Hal, saw to it I survived a cataclysm to ensure the survival of my twins. Yet to this day an awful truth remains: If not for Raven and Constantia's desperate need for their mother, I would have closed my eyes the moment I shot Giselle never to open them again.

4

Solitude on a sea island was not what I had in mind when I first returned to Charleston. I arrived pregnant though with little idea of how such a condition would drive things, and I do mean all things. The initial stage of my plan, that of living in one of the old Peregrine cottages on Sullivan's Island, worked out well enough. But the next stage, working five days a week in Mr. Pinckney's law office, fell apart the second month in. It happened the morning a nurse called from my obstetrician's office and told me I was carrying twins. On learning this momentous news, Mr. Pinckney rose from his desk chair and made a lordly speech. He declared he could no longer stand the stress of watching me overdo. Then he insisted I retreat to the beach cottage for the duration of my pregnancy and as long thereafter as I needed.

"It is my deliberated opinion," he said, "a woman in a condition as delicate as yours ought to quit work altogether and concentrate on the problem at hand, that of hatching out two healthy chicks."

Three weeks into my confinement (Mr. Pinckney's word), it dawned on me that turning one of the cottage's three bedrooms into a nursery was not enough to satisfy my workaholic addiction to pressure. Lounging in the porch swing day after day made my head feel mushier than the pumpkin my abdomen was beginning to resemble. I needed more than curtains and crib pads to keep my mind alert. Project possibilities paraded through my head: poetry chapbooks, cross-stitched scenes of nursery rhymes, antique furniture restoration, cooking lessons, all of which I rejected. They seemed too difficult for a pumpkin head to manage.

Then one morning while staring at the *Charleston Post & Courier* without assimilating much in the way of news, my eyes fell upon a last-ditch student recruitment ad run by The Citadel. I say last-ditch since most classes for the summer term would begin within the week. I read the ad with unusual interest for someone about to enter the most difficult phase of her life. My vision of the changes two infants would bring to daily living remained, let us say, underdeveloped.

We have your future at The Citadel, read the ad. Enroll for summer term. Education courses count toward teacher certification and renewal.

"Certification," I said aloud. "Teacher certification." The words appeared to grow larger on the page each time I blinked. When their font size reached eighteen, an epiphany burst forth in my pumpkin head. This is it, I thought. My project. I'll go back to college. I'll become a certified teacher. Then I can work in the same building with my twins when they are old enough to go to school. Our lives will be perfect. I'll be the ideal mother.

You don't have to tell me how wrong I was. It took a little while, but eventually I realized that as epiphanies go, this one was half-baked. How could it be anything else? I had yet to meet up with contractions, childbirth, colic, crying, bottles, wet diapers, wet everything, or with the excruciating brand of sleep deprivation known only to new parents.

Instead, I saw laid out before me the happy delusion of a picturesque future. I would become a mother and a certified teacher in one broad stroke never again to have to grovel about as an uncertified, underpaid, part-time instructor. Despite my advancing age and sketchy background, I would achieve the status of a professional educator, a real teacher licensed by the state. I became giddy at the prospect of embarking at the same time upon two such noble endeavors as motherhood and teaching. It did not occur to me that anyone with even the slightest knowledge of my personality and temperament would have advised me against involvement in either.

After lunch on the day of said epiphany, I drove my Explorer SUV – the one concession I had made to middle-class values since my return to the Holy City – to the campus of The Citadel, where I talked the Dean of the Education Department into allowing me to enroll in two graduate level education courses before completing the university admissions process. (Long story.)

"I'll finish my paperwork by the end of the week," I said. "And if I don't, you can drop me from both class rolls."

The lifelong bureaucrat peered at me over half-glasses and did not appear to like what he saw in the area beneath my rib cage. "Highly irregular," he said as he scratched out two override admit slips and thrust them in my direction. "Women expect so much these days. Highly irregular."

I left the dean's office dazed. I had taken my first step ever toward participation in something of social value, the shoes of which already felt tight. To my heretofore shallow way of thinking, the profession of teaching shared characteristics with other professions I considered missionary in nature – social work, nursing, counseling. And here I was joining this selfless throng of do-gooders like some newly evangelized cultist, hands lifted high in the air, pupils dilated, mouth fixed in ecstatic grin.

I did not recognize myself. Nor did I anticipate the hardships I would encounter along this road-less-traveled, hardships made far more difficult for the mother of two small children. I don't know why I did not consider the length of the process, or how unlikely it was I would ever finish. If I had appreciated fully what I was getting into, I'd have run out of the dean's office screaming instead of bouncing out with gladness.

It took the brightness of sunlight to illuminate my new undertaking. I did not expect to feel intimidated by what I thought was going to be a simple, early childhood education program of study.

But as I stood on the sidewalk outside Capers Hall on the campus of The Citadel, flipping through the catalogue of requirements the dean had taken such sadistic pleasure in laying upon me, I crashed from my high.

I did feel intimidated...very. What was going on here? A person had to do all this to become a certified teacher? My level of respect for those in the profession rose higher with every description of every requirement about which I read. Did all the teachers at Southern Prep – those poor exhausted souls I considered myself better than – go through this same impossible progression...page after page of research projects, courses, practicums, experiences in real schools, on-site observations, and, finally, the biggest bear of all...student teaching?

The weighty catalogue came close to squeezing every drop of joy out of my shiny new venture. But then one of the twins yanked me back to the present with a sharp kick to the bladder. I smiled and became a pumpkin head again. And so it happened that a case of muddled thinking drove my life-changing decision not to trash the Education Department's Catalogue-of-Bad-News on that morning or any other.

5

Helpless and exhausted, I lay back in the birthing chair and listened to the obstetrician as she chattered to my second newborn.

"Hello, blondie," she said. "Guess your mom won't hold it against you – hey, stop wiggling so much – for causing her to miss her Kiddie Lit class this morning. Hold still, let me wash your face. You want to be spiffy when you meet your mother. Can't let your sister steal all the thunder being born first."

I rallied when I heard my baby mewing. "Are you sure she's okay?" I said. "Ten fingers, ten toes?"

"Perfection, just what the ultrasound promised. Here, take a peek."

She handed my baby to the waiting nurse who swaddled her in a pink blanket and slipped a knit cap onto her tiny head before placing her in my arms. "Oh, look at you," I said to the squinty little face. "How sweet you are. How pink. You're worth missing every class ever taught."

I held my child close and laughed in spite of my weariness. Then I slid off her cap and kissed the top of her head. "And your hair, blond. How can that be? Your sister's hair is so dark."

"Fraternal twins," the doctor said, "no more alike than any other sisters. Her father had a blond gene for sure, and you contributed one of your own from somewhere in that Italian background. Light hair is recessive. Both parents have to ante up a gene for it. What's her name? I heard you call the other one Raven."

"I was wrong," I said, turning my baby over to examine the back of her head. Ringlets still damp from the doctor's baby-wipe lay in swirls from nape to crown. I stroked the soft strands with my fingertips to encourage their natural curl. "This one is Raven," I murmured. "The dark-haired one is Constantia."

⌘ ⌘ ⌘

You will be surprised to learn that before the twins made their debut, I somehow managed to turn in every piece of paperwork required for admission to the graduate school at The Citadel, plus finish the first two courses in my program. But after the arrival of my babies, the word derailed comes to mind. I had to drop out of my third course altogether. What did you say? Why would a woman sign up for a graduate class so close to her due date? I would offer you a reasonable explanation if I had one.

Why, indeed? Ignorance? Superwoman syndrome? Denial? Speculating, I'd say all of the above. The only thing I can report with real accuracy is that a year...no, two years...whooshed by without my thinking about course work of any kind.

Motherhood consumed me. I spent every ounce of my time and energy striving for perfection, but – and I can assure you of this beyond doubt – if Tycie had not come to help me, I would not have made it through the first month. I give her full credit for the splendid manner in which Raven and Constantia thrived. I did the best I could...always...but on most days my best was not enough. I needed Tycie's brand of wisdom. So did Raven and Constantia. Without it, all three of us would have sunk.

6

Perhaps you would like to know how it came about that Tycie got dropped on my doorstep at the critical hour. Once again, I have Grayson Pinckney to thank. A week after the twins were born, Mr. Pinckney dispatched his dignified chauffeur, Caesar, to Roper Hospital to collect me and my little ones and drive us home to Sullivan's. After which he and Caesar made a roundtrip to Edisto Island to fetch Tycie. Any excuse sufficed for Mr. Pinckney to visit his ancestral home if for no more than a drive-by. But when he and Caesar got back to Sullivan's with Tycie in tow, and saw my condition when I answered the door, he knew – all three gray-heads knew – their arrival was barely ahead of disaster. By then I was so close to the end of my rope that I thought for a wild moment Mr. Pinckney's expectation was for me to take care of Tycie, not the other way around.

The three visiting angels – Mr. Pinckney, Caesar, and Tycie – did not wait to be invited inside, a good thing since I was too frazzled to remember anything as ordinary as manners. Both babies were yowling demands for everything at once from a mother depleted of strength. Mr. Pinckney leveled an offended look at the bawling Constantia in my arms. I patted her tiny back, but could not console her. I suppose I had forgotten about Raven bawling in her bassinet.

The Pinckney patriarch yelled at me above the racket. "Hello, hello, you poor suffering soul. Caterwauling of this magnitude tells me I was right. A new mother of your modern type is bound to have need of some old-fashioned assistance. We are the mercy brigade come to intervene in desperate times."

It was then I noticed that Caesar was hefting a rocking chair, and Tycie a worn-out suitcase. Mr. Pinckney hefted nothing heavier than his walking stick. I stepped aside and watched Caesar wrestle the rocker into the living room and plunk it down next to the smaller one already there.

"Thank you, my good man," said Mr. Pinckney. "Two babies need two rockers. I don't know why Miss Roz and I didn't think of that sooner, perhaps because Honor is an only child. Now then, Tycie has come to stay a while. She is going to occupy the rocker Caesar just brought in. It came from Pinckney House downtown, and Tycie is familiar with its creak. She had the pleasure of rocking two generations of Pinckney progeny in that same chair on her days off from Peregrine House."

Gladness flooded my soul as Tycie shuffled over and picked up the crying Raven who immediately burrowed into the old woman's bosom and fell asleep. Mr. Pinckney lowered his voice though not enough to help my headache.

"Yes, yes, yes," he said. "Arlena, my dear, you are a lucky woman. Mrs. Roosevelt has expressed a willingness to minister to you in your time of need, a true Godsend, for I myself am unwilling. So is Caesar. No male animal in his right mind would put up with two babies squalling at the same time. I hope the angry little creatures you are harboring here get to be twenty-one years of age before I next lay eyes on them. I bid them goodbye and good riddance."

He and Caesar then departed, leaving Tycie and me on our own with the two angry little creatures. And for all intents and purposes, that is how things remained the next two years until the day Tycie emerged from the guest bedroom and declared she needed to go back to Edisto to take care of Daddy Abraham in his dotage, an untrue statement if I ever heard one. She was not walking out on me to tend Daddy Abraham. The fact was that Tycie did not like the tone of a certain telephone conversation she had overheard between Stuart and me on Raven and Constantia's second birthday. She had to hear only my end to know she disapproved. I hadn't bothered to discuss with her my decision to inform Stuart he was the father of twins. I guess I should not have been surprised when she took it as her cue to exit. No rational person would have wanted to endure the avalanche of unpleasantness a phone call like that was bound to set in motion. I implored her to stay to no avail. Her repeated response was a stylized, wordless gesture - the straightening of her back accompanied by the pointing of an arthritic forefinger in the direction of the cottage next door, residence of my neighbor and friend, Hettie Lupio, another beloved grandma-type who had already proven her competence at childcare.

But I was not ready to give up on Tycie. I humiliated myself by weeping and begging in the face of her resolve. Exasperated, she found her voice again. "It's like Mr. Pinckney told you. You are a lucky woman. Missy Lupio is good people."

Tycie shared this platitude with me as she was packing her bag to leave me alone with the angry little creatures, though her facial expression in no way matched her words. Frowning hard, she closed her suitcase and continued blessing me with several more opinions I did not want to hear. "Missy Lupio can do whatever needs doing around here. She loves little ones. Told me she raised four of her own and half-raised six grands. So quit your complaining. All you have to do is pay her what you've been paying me, and everything will go smooth as ebb tide...if you take my advice, that is, and stop yapping on the phone with that long-lost husband of yours. I know you've been making plans for him to visit your babies. You best be careful encouraging a thing like that. You don't know him anymore. He could jump up and turn into a problem."

"Stuart?" I said. "He's not the problem. You are...leaving us by ourselves. Stuart's interest in the girls will be short-lived and no help. I guarantee it. But we can't make it five minutes without you."

She gave me another disgusted look before putting me in my place the last time. "If you let a man you don't trust, not even enough to live with, come slinking into your children's lives, you'll have to make it without me. Missy Lupio ain't got rheumatism. She's modern for an old woman, the kind that won't be upset by the fancy new word you been throwing around on the phone… vi-si-tation. You'll be one regretful little mother hen if you let your baby chicks out from under your wing too soon."

"But he's their father. Surely you can't think they'd be better off not knowing him."

"Not if he'd been in the picture their whole lives, but he hasn't. There's plenty of time down the road for vi-si-tation. Your babies are too young to be shuffled back and forth. And you've got no business consorting with a man who treated you so bad you had to leave him. It's senseless turning your back on your children when they can't fend for themselves. Even a mama cat knows better. What's the matter with you?"

I had no more answers, and Tycie had no more questions. She snorted her final disapproval, picked up her suitcase by its leather grip, and changed her tone from accusatory to gloomy. "I'm going back to Edisto where I belong, to Freedmen's Village and Daddy Abraham. My grandson, Abe, is coming directly to pick me up in his automobile. Lord only knows I can't do no more good here. But when I get to my own bedside, I'm going to kneel and pray for you and your two young'uns."

My tone went gloomy as well. "Stuart is their father, Tycie. What choice do I have?"

"Don't let your little ones go, child. They'll forget you. You'll forget them. I know you're tired and your heart feels dry, but if you keep going through the motions of pouring love on your children, someday a good man will come along and pour a little love on you. A new man, not that old one. I know you claim you don't need a man's love no more. But Tycie knows a lie when she hears one. Keep your children close a little longer and mind your wounded heart. If you don't, your soul's gonna wither and die."

I wish I had heeded Tycie's warnings. I wish I had allowed myself to believe love could transcend human weakness and harmonize with the souls of children…my children…real love that was no metaphor for God, but God himself. Why did I think I had no birthright to love? Why did I not listen to God's voice speaking to me through Tycie?

7

"Oatmeal, oatmeal. Always with the oatmeal. You girls are going to turn into bowls of this mush if you keep eating it every day. Why can't you be like other children and eat junk food for breakfast? Here, drink your orange juice. I have to stir the lumps out of this goop."

I leaned over and demanded kisses in exchange for juice from my two sleepy four-year-olds. Raven threw her arms around my neck and gave me more sticky love than I bargained for, the jolt of which caused my hand to jiggle. "Hey," I said. "I'm spilling juice on your sister."

Constantia primped her mouth to cry when a splash of orange hit her cheek. Raven saw and jumped to her aid the same way she always did when her twin sister encountered a problem. "Don't cry, Connie," she said. "I'll wipe it off with my napkin."

I watched Raven minister to Constantia and tried to remember the precise time she had begun exhibiting this pattern of behavior. I could not recall, reason being the beginning did not occur this side of the womb. I suspected Raven was taking care of Constantia before they were ever born.

A menacing glup from the cookpot pulled me back to the present. I was amazed by my own behavior – me, the non-cook, standing over steaming porridge every morning. The transformations motherhood had brought about in a liberated woman were astonishing to behold. I had almost mastered laundry.

I gave the oatmeal a last quick stir before dishing it into Cinderella bowls and setting them in front of Raven and Constantia. Whereupon they began the important tasks of blowing away steam and testing the temperature. As they were about to take their first bites, the wall phone rang. Raven pushed her bowl aside and scrambled to her knees on the wobbly bar stool. I grabbed her elbow to steady her as she stretched to pluck the receiver from its cradle. Her face brightened when she heard the caller's voice.

"Daddy," she said, elated. I sighed with displeasure. Raven, clever little kitten that she was, purred into the phone. "Uh-huh, Mama's here. She made oatmeal…said we were going to turn into bowls of it, but I'd rather be the sugar bowl in Cinderella. It can sing and dance."

I held out my hand for the receiver, fingers waggling, face severe. Raven ignored me and chattered on. She always turned up the charm for Stuart, the infrequent caller and more infrequent visitor…Santa Claus daddy. I in dreary contrast remained comfy old mom. And as all four-year-olds know, comfy old moms need no wooing.

"Give me the phone, please," I said, my voice gruff on purpose. "You don't want Constantia to eat your breakfast."

Raven made a pout mouth and betrayed me. "Mama wants to talk," she whispered into the phone. "She's got her mad face on."

I felt my cheeks flush at my child's disloyalty. Unknowing and uncaring, she shoved the receiver toward me and repositioned her small backside on the stool.

"Eat," I said to her before acknowledging Stuart on the phone. "I'll make jelly toast to go with your oatmeal if you're quiet while I talk to Daddy."

Raven laughed and bopped her sister on the shoulder. "Eat," she said. "Mommy's going to make us six million jelly toasts."

Constantia, busy with her spoon, paid her sister no attention. I grimaced, took a cleansing breath, and spoke curtly into the receiver. "Stuart, I've already told you, mornings aren't good for calls. I'm trying to get everybody ready for playschool."

"Don't hang up on me, Arly. Why did you take Connie off? I didn't get a chance to tell her I love her."

"That was Raven. Don't you know your own children? Look, if you're trying to make me mad, you're succeeding. I have to maintain a semblance of order around here, by myself. Long distance parenting is a crock. Aunt Lucia tried to tell me that after my own parents took off. Now I know what she was talking about. Why don't you and Giselle focus on your sophisticated lives in Boston and leave child rearing to me?"

"We're not in Boston. We're here, downtown at the Belmond. Flew in last night."

"What? You aren't due for a visit, not for three more weeks."

"I don't want to wait that long. Giselle is downstairs in the lobby arranging for a rental car. Counters weren't open at the airport when we got in. We're driving out to Sullivan's."

I stopped in the middle of my one-handed task of buttering Constantia's toast, Tycie's warning echoing in my brain. It was past time to set Stuart straight on what he and Giselle could and could not do. I knew what they wanted, and I knew what they were not going to get. I intended to prove Tycie wrong.

"You're wasting your time," I said. "The girls are in playschool all week, and I have an important class at The Citadel this morning. I'm finishing up my last required course before student teaching starts, no cuts allowed. And Saturday, let me think, Saturday… Saturday. That's no good, either. The girls are invited to a birthday party for a classmate. And Sunday we're going to the annual dinner-on-the-ground picnic at Tycie's church on Edisto. What makes you think I'd cancel any of those plans? You and Giselle can't show up on a whim and expect everyone to jump to your tune."

Raven widened her eyes on hearing Stuart was close by. "I want to see Daddy," she said and punched Constantia to join in. "We want to see Daddy."

I dropped the toast and cupped my hand over the receiver. "Quiet…Mommy can't hear. If you want cookies in your snack bag, stop that right now."

But they didn't stop that right now. They continued in a whisper. "We want to see Daddy." I looked at them in despair. If a brick wall had been nearby, I would have banged my head against it.

"You're out of line, Stuart," I said into the phone. "Now I'm dealing with a power struggle here. Stop with the morning phone calls."

"Don't hang up…don't. More visitation isn't too much to ask, not when you've had Raven and Connie their whole lives. They were two years old before you even told me they existed. And now Giselle and I…"

I hung up on him in mid-sentence like he knew I would. The phone rang three more times while I was trying to finish getting the girls fed and dressed. And each time my angry little creatures chanted anew. "We want to see Daddy."

I retaliated by not answering the phone.

8

It was nine fifteen by the time I turned the girls over to their playschool teacher, Mrs. Burton. Raven, all innocent eyes and bee-stung lips, clung to my skirt and looked up at the matron whose mean poker face suggested she should have been excelling in the profession of criminal justice instead of failing in the profession of teaching. Raven batted her eyelashes and announced she and Constantia were late to school because, "Mommy and Daddy were fighting on the phone."

Mrs. Poker-Face gave me a dirty look as she ushered my children into the sanctuary of her classroom where I'm certain Raven wasted no time filling her in on the details of our morning.

The twins' playschool was in the education space of Sullivan's Island Baptist Church on Central Avenue. My custom was to walk them to school the three short blocks from the cottage in deference to what I thought charming life on a barrier island should look like. But on this morning, I chauffeured them in the SUV since I had to be in Mount Pleasant at nine to pick up my printer from the repair shop.

After dropping the girls off, I returned to the Explorer and spent a moment digging through my purse for my cell. I don't know why. I was sick of the thing. It had not stopped ringing and vibrating since breakfast. I had finally turned the ringer off in self-defense, the result of which was a voice mailbox full of messages from Stuart. I took pleasure in deleting them without listening to a single one. Then noting the time on my phone screen, I started the engine of the Explorer and headed, a bit too fast for charming island life, toward the Ben Sawyer Bridge and Mt. Pleasant. My plan was to retrieve my printer and get back to the cottage in haste. I wanted to finish my assignment for class before unwanted visitors, namely, Stuart and Giselle, got organized enough to show up and break my concentration.

I should have known better than to think I could perform such a miracle. They were waiting for me in the driveway when I got back, suave Stuart and smug Giselle, sweating it out in the front seat of a Kodak yellow rented Mercedes. I spied them before they spied me. They were busy scoping out the cottage like two real estate sharpies preparing to fleece the owner. Mr. Pinckney and I were the only ones who knew the cottage did not belong to me free and clear, that it was part of Miss Peregrine's estate. Though why I enjoyed letting Stuart believe otherwise, I do not know. Maybe I wanted him to think I had fared better without him, that my life was now rosy instead of beige. More importantly, why did I think he would care? He was into millions now, Giselle's millions.

I parked close to the back steps as far from the Mercedes as I could get, which deterred Stuart and Giselle not at all. By the time I switched off the Explorer's engine, they were out of their own vehicle and striding toward mine. I jerked up the emergency brake and slid from under the steering wheel. I had no time for jabberwocky. My priority was to unload the printer and get started on my assignment, not stand around making nice with unwanted callers. I marched to the back of the Explorer and pressed the cargo-door button. It took effort to dislodge the awkward printer. And when I turned around with it gripped in my hands, I startled at Stuart and Giselle's proximity.

"Get out of my way," I said. "This thing is heavy. It's the old kind, retro."

Stuart stepped forward. "Let me carry it. You'll never make it up the steps."

"I made it down; I'll make it back up…if you'll move." I began my determined trudge toward the stairway, complaining and staggering as I went. "If you came to continue tormenting me about extra visitation, the answer is still no. And stop calling here mornings. It's hard enough to keep a routine going without your interference. I haven't had regular help since Tycie two years ago. And that's your fault, too."

Stuart ignored my rant. He had his own agenda. "Raven and Constantia love it when I call. They groove on attention from their dad."

I lumbered on toward the stairs, the antique printer digging into my forearms. First stair-step: "What they groove on is your consumer orientation which stinks to high heaven. On the way to school this morning, Raven told Constantia you were taking them to a big fancy hotel with a pool and ordering ice cream for lunch like last time."

Second stair-step: "I get it that you and Giselle don't care if I wear myself out making fruit cups and yogurt smoothies for their lunches. Raven and Constantia don't care, either. They would rather have ice cream. But mean old Mommy makes them eat nourishing food. She worries about the development of their bones and teeth. Meanwhile, Daddy and Giselle buy their affection with sugar on a regular basis. Why is that, Stuart?"

Giselle pretended not to understand the concept of the rhetorical question, or perhaps she did not have to pretend. She opened her mouth to speak, but Stuart stopped her by stating a fact that pleased her and infuriated me.

"Arlena, you know very well that Raven and Constantia would not have known we were in town if you hadn't let it slip on the phone."

Third stair-step: "Whatever," I said. "You're the one who called before eight and got them going, then left me to deal with the fallout. I'm asking you plain and simple, back off."

Fourth stair-step: "And as for showing up in Charleston with no notice expecting more visitation. Forget it. You won't find a judge anywhere who'll put up with you harassing me like this. Your haphazard way of doing things is the reason I can't bring myself to trust you with visits longer than a weekend? If you and what's-her-face..." – I sent Giselle a contemptuous look – "...were as concerned for the girls as yourselves, I wouldn't feel so uneasy."

Giselle, unused to being insulted and denied, could keep quiet no longer. And this time Stuart failed at bridling her. "You're nothing but selfish," she said out of a slit of a mouth made lip-less by its owner's rush of anger. The big money she had spent on designer makeup was a loss of investment that morning. Stuart had let this little spending habit of hers drop during a phone conversation one evening when he and his new bride were on the outs.

Giselle honked on like a Canadian goose. "Stuart says you were so greedy when you and he were married that you hid money from him. I think you're afraid the girls might love us more than you. And my name is Giselle, not what's-her-face...Giselle Marie Bordeau Prince. That's French, if you didn't know."

A hundred scathing remarks jetted through my mind – I know your name is French, Giselle. But I don't care. You have poodle breath and a case of the frizzies and lipstick on your teeth, probably because there's nowhere else to smear it since you have no lips. And your new husband is a perfect baudet, French for jackass.

I managed to refrain from saying any of those things though not out of maturity. Oh, no, never that. My intent was to cut Giselle more deeply with the sharp blade of silence.

9

Time was I would have attacked with claws and fists anyone who talked down to me about Raven and Constantia. The childless Giselle, having no natural maternal instincts, did not comprehend that my concern was genuine, not some trumped-up pretense. Judging from her actions and speech, I felt sure she had convinced herself my primary motivation was to keep the upper hand. But that was not it. I craved harmony, not dissonance. It hurt me to be dragged along the path of discord. And the sad fact was that Stuart had less excuse than Giselle for putting the twins at risk. He was their biological father. Nevertheless he stirred up trouble at every turn. I gave Giselle a pass. After all, she was not blood kin. To me, she was no more than a hobbyist, a collector of trinkets, to include little children if a pretty pair wandered into her line of vision.

I often found myself frustrated, not so much by Giselle herself, but our inability to communicate. It was disheartening to be hit again and again with the sad reality we would never be able to join hearts in the mothering of Raven and Constantia. I considered

Giselle a narcissist, and I'm sure she considered worse about me. Perhaps we were both correct. Perhaps we were staring into opposite sides of a horror house mirror. I found her unwholesome interest in Raven and Constantia alarming and Stuart's interest worse, his constant banging on about how he wanted to be with his children…deserved for them to know him as their father…felt I owed it to him to make that possible.

In rational moments, I was able to acknowledge the impact of my own past actions. It was true. Stuart did not know how to be a proper father because I had not allowed him sufficient practice. My stinginess with visitation had put a strain on everyone, including Giselle. But Stuart and his new wife's comfort level, or lack thereof, was not important to me. I had to stay in control. How else could I make sure Raven and Constantia's wellbeing remained at the top of everyone's priority list?

But the more I said no to extra visitation, the more Stuart ramped up his demands. His persistence chilled my heart. So did Giselle's. Emotion, not logic, charged her interest. Ruthlessness charged Stuart's. He had no qualms about exposing anyone's sensitive places if it would get him what he wanted, not even his new bride's. If he and Giselle were in a fight, he would call me and attack her behind her back, discredit her, reveal the sources of her pain. I was surprised to hear how commonplace they were: her inability to have children, anxiety about my and Stuart's old relationship, a debilitating need to possess things, and, most troublesome of all, an inflated sense of entitlement that had resulted in a bored-little-rich-girl growing up to become a bored-little-rich-woman.

I was wrong to think Stuart's emotional disloyalty to Giselle gave me an advantage. Why did I not remember he could turn loyalty on and off as easily as water from a tap? If I had, perhaps I'd have been less shocked when he told me he and Giselle thought the girls would be better off living with them instead of me. I listened, speechless, as he went into detail over the phone about Giselle's heart being in the right place, and if she were their biological mother, she would sacrifice anything, to the point of giving them up entirely, to ensure they would have the experience of a real family with both father and mother figures in the home.

His pompous lecture spawned the first in a series of debilitating quarrels on the subject. Misunderstandings boiled over on both sides. But as I said, I held the sole-custody card which guaranteed my position. I honestly believed I had nothing to lose by closing the door in Stuart's face.

I know what you are thinking at this point. Tycie's advice had been true and good. I should have listened when she warned me against inviting problems with no solutions into the lives of my children. Now I know she was right. But how was I to know then... before I made the series of horrendous decisions that unleashed the deadly storm?

10

Heavy printer still in hand, I forced myself up to the fifth stair-step before stopping to rest. How had my simple plan gone so wrong? All I wanted was a few hours of solitude to finish my course assignment. My arms ached from the weight of the printer, my heart from the aggression of Stuart and Giselle.

I looked down at my two adversaries. Auras shimmered all around them, hellish forewarnings of another of my debilitating headaches. I stared into Giselle's defiant eyes in an effort to see inside the soul of a woman who thought it acceptable to take another woman's children. Her pink outfit did not go with her pinched face. She looked unhappy despite her expensive dress, the hem of which fluttered about her knees. My own sadness deepened as I studied her, yearning as I often did for a perfect world in which she and I could communicate like proper adults for the sake of Raven and Constantia. Hello, my name is Arlena. What's yours? Ah, Giselle...a lovely name. French, isn't it? Très belle.

But for this perfect world there was no hope. Fate had cast us as rivals – bitter ex-wife versus saccharin new wife; exhausted biological mother versus energetic stepmother; dark-on-dark versus bright-on-bright – with neither of us having a say in the matter.

I shifted the printer in my arms. Could Stuart not see I was about to fall down the stairs? Though he would not have cared if I had broken my neck, not when on a mission to serve himself. I blinked. The little strength I had left was waning. I tried to focus, but failed. Turning my attention back to the higher steps, I made it up one more to the accompaniment of Giselle bleating at me from below. Her words assaulted my eardrums. "You're jealous," she said, "'cause the girls like us best."

I did not respond. I was too exhausted to think of a smart comeback. In college, I had developed the art of sarcasm, but had given it up on becoming a mother. I did not want to be unworthy.

"Wait, Arlena," Stuart said. Giselle had already exhausted her vocabulary, which took four seconds max. (Please, don't call my hand on sarcasm for that last small observation. I was merely stating a fact, sharing a piece of information about the new love of Stuart's life.)

I knew from the thud of his feet on the stairway that Stuart was about to run into me from behind. "Please…talk to us," he said directly into my ear. I felt his breath, smelled his morning coffee. "No pressure, just talk. We can work this out. I know we can."

Near tears, I turned and stared into his eyes. Maybe I should be more civil, I thought. He looks old and tired, wrinkled even. I wonder if he knows.

I was about to say out loud that it might be a good idea for a man his age to stop frequenting tanning parlors, but I did not get the chance. Giselle was now stealing the show, teetering up the steps behind Stuart on her pink stilettos that looked to have been dyed in the same vat as her dress. I watched in amazement as her right ankle gave way, requiring her to claw at Stuart's left shoulder to stay upright. Her dignity flew away on the same gust of wind as my civility. Where did Stuart find this woman? I did not know there was enough money in the universe to make fuchsia toenails with white French tips tolerable to a man with his snooty tastes.

Disbelief in my eyes, I shifted my gaze from Giselle's toes back to Stuart's face that was now maroon with embarrassment. I did not have to speak a word. He knew what I was thinking. Why in the name of sense are you with this woman?

I pitied him as he used facial expression alone to beg mercy. Giselle in all her glory had burned away his confabulated self and replaced it with pathetic reality. I took advantage of his weakness. "Here's the way it's going to be," I hissed, enjoying the one moment of power that had fallen my way for the entire morning. (Now then...to get the best effects from this ridiculous scene you must continue to picture Giselle hanging onto Stuart's shoulder from behind, grinding her gold-capped molars, blinking her extended eyelashes rapidly enough to create a breeze; and me with my signature out-of-control hair and no makeup. I did, however, remain in the lead on huffiness and articulation.) "I'll talk this over with you, Stuart, but not with her…never."

From the corner of my eye, I saw the silky sleeve of Giselle's Giambattista Fali dress flapping in a gust of wind off the ocean. It was distracting, but not enough to stop me from lobbing a fresh volley of mean rhetoric toward Stuart. "You and I both know what's-her-face isn't interested in Raven and Constantia's welfare. How could anyone who's not blood kin? Which, I grant you, isn't her fault. So…if you can get her to wait a couple of minutes in that monstrosity of a vehicle over there, I'll set this printer down and listen to whatever you have to say. But only you, Stuart, you alone."

He closed his eyes. His right cheek twitched. He knew Giselle would stomp his sandaled feet to bloody pulps with the heels of her stilettos if he made such a suggestion. Our conversation was over. Victorious Giselle (victorious over what, I did not know) let go of Stuart's shoulder and bumbled her way down the steps. The last I saw of her, she was clacking toward the Mercedes, her ankles bending this way and that above the instruments-of-torture strapped to her feet. It was clear her expectation was for Stuart to follow. Which he did due to basic cowardice, but not before shoving a folded note into the paper tray of the printer. I let him get away with this silly indiscretion out of compassion (yeah, right, ha!). What I was really thinking was...what kind of worm has this man become? Secret notes? Tanning parlors? Pedicured male toes peeping out between leather strips of expensive Italian sandals? Giselle would have skewered him if she had known what he was up to. I felt like skewering him myself.

As the yellow monster roared north on Atlantic Avenue, I hobbled my way up the remaining steps and through the back door to the kitchen. Where I stopped to catch my breath a few seconds before continuing on to the sunroom. As I lowered my burden onto the ponderosa table, several seashells cracked under its weight. They were treasures Raven and Constantia had brought in from the beach the day before. I made a mental note to clear away the evidence before the shell owners came home at lunchtime and discovered their destruction.

Stuart's note taunted me from the printer tray. I jerked it out, unfolded and read it aloud. Three o'clock today, the Hangover Club. Please!

Men, I thought with disdain. Don't they ever grow up?

11

I called Mrs. Lupio, my seventy-year-old neighbor who had replaced Tycie as my go-to when I needed help with the girls. She never said no to my requests, this time for three hours of babysitting. It pleased me when she asked for four. She said an art project was in the offing and the artist (herself) needed the help of two young assistants.

Mrs. Lupio's cottage doubled as her home and studio. Raven and Constantia considered it an enchanted castle for little girls. When I told them they were going there to play, they ran shouting into their bedroom and jumped up and down on their beds. Hettie Lupio's turbans, flowing caftans, and endless supply of art materials fascinated them, almost as much as twins who looked nothing alike fascinated Hettie Lupio. She referred to them as her odd little duo. "What kind of twins," she would say, "don't resemble each other in the least?"

Not long after the girls progressed beyond toddler stage, Mrs. Lupio painted a watercolor series of her little neighbors – Raven, angel-faced in a Charleston bonnet; Constantia, bare-shouldered in a white eyelet slip; together in sky-blue sun-suits, laughing and bouncing barefoot on the joggling board that dominated Mrs. Lupio's back deck. The aging artist titled the series Belle Sorelle (Beautiful Sisters) and hung the paintings on the walls of her studio. And, yes, they are still there.

On the afternoon I was to meet Stuart at the Hangover (like the chump I was), I walked Raven and Constantia over to Mrs. Lupio's cottage and answered the same question the lady-of-the-studio always asked: "Arlena, darling, are you certain they gave you the right babies at the hospital? Maybe there's a misplaced child in the world somewhere who resembles one of these?"

"No mistake," I said, "but you have a long-lost twin, Mrs. Lupio. Except for a few years difference in age, your mirror image lives in Texas, my college roommate, Rennie. She's just like you - looks, temperament, artistic bent, everything. Did your hair happen to be red before it turned white?"

"Redder than a cherry," said the artist.

Raven squealed and clapped her hands at the cherry metaphor. Constantia looked thoughtful, her response to everything no matter how ordinary. After a moment of reflection, she said, "Maybe Mrs. Lupio and Aunt Rennie really are twins, like Raven and me."

"Yes," shouted Raven. "Twin cherries on top of twin cones of ice cream."

Mrs. Lupio laughed and adjusted her turban. "You might be able to convince me of that," she said, "except our birthdays are decades apart. Come outside on the deck, both of you. I'm working with natural clay this afternoon. Are there any curious children around who'd like to make models of baby loggerhead and paint them green with brown spots?"

Mrs. Lupio had the patience for projects with Raven and Constantia that I intended to tackle but never seemed to find time. When I left my girls with Hettie Lupio, they might decorate paper dragons with glitter and glue, string yarn necklaces with seashells, make handprints and footprints in plaster, or, as on this lovely afternoon, fashion baby loggerheads out of clay. It made me happy to see my twins fall under her spell. I knew it would cause the departure of their mother to go unnoticed. But then, so would her return, which hurt my feelings every time.

12

Don't tell me I was foolish to meet Stuart at a bar. I'm aware...now anyway. Back then, I don't know. It seemed reasonable in a way after being schooled by every pop-culture article in existence that with-it women of the sort I made myself out to be should work with ex-husbands for the sake of the children.

As I drove the bridges and roadways to the ill-conceived meeting, I wondered if Stuart had anything other than fatherhood on his mind. Nothing to do with romance, I hoped. Secret meetings, indeed. Had he always been this superficial? Had I missed it somehow in the old days?

I found his choice of venue insulting, though I knew the reason behind it. He was trying to avoid the crosshairs of Giselle's fury. It was easy to read his assumptions – new wife, Giselle, would never soil her pink, Gucci pumps by exposing them to the gritty floor of the Hangover Club, but ex-wife, Arlena, wouldn't mind dirtying up her knock-off espadrilles, not anywhere.

To be fair, he was right. Giselle, reigning queen of purchased style, worked hard at maintaining her collection of Prada-and-such. I, on the other hand, owned no Prada-and-such to maintain. Therefore, peanut shells on a bar room floor presented no problem for me. Nor to Stuart. He owned no Prada, either.

I wanted to believe, if inaccurately, that destiny had brought me to the Hangover's front door. I wanted to, but could not. The actuality of the bar's dingy entrance made me wish I had not fallen prey to Stuart's cajoling. He had called my cell on the sly after the drama skit with Giselle back at the cottage. I'd listened without sympathy as he begged me with a fake tremor in his voice to give him one last chance to plead his case. "Please, just meet me," he'd said. "I promise, no rancor. It'll be easy…like old times."

Thus, in line with my new and practiced role as soft-hearted pushover, the role I had adopted on becoming a mother (stop rolling your eyes), I caved in. But on observing the electric-blue paint that was peeling in flaky strips off the door of a bar I had not seen the inside of in years, I regretted being such a sweetheart.

I won't go in, I thought. I'll stand him up. He can sit in this filthy cave and drink himself blind, and I will never show. Snatching his wadded note from of my purse, I threw it at the beer-perfumed trashcan beside the door. It bounced off the edge and fell to the ground amidst all the other litter. My lack of aim annoyed me. I suspected Tycie was somehow aware of the trouble I was experiencing. Of course, she was. She had predicted it. But as big a mistake as I knew it was, I had told Stuart I would talk with him, if for no other reason than to put a stop to his harassment. And what other way could we discuss anything except in person? His whining over the phone grated on my nerves so badly - the wheedling, beseeching, finagling to get his way. Or was it Giselle's way? I felt like killing Stuart (a terrifying omen, though I did not realize its significance until way later) when he moaned and groaned on call after call about how much he missed Raven and Constantia, missed being a real father to them, spending time with them, enjoying and loving them.

But his pestering on the phone compared in no way to being double-teamed by him and his new wifey in my own driveway. That was when I realized I needed permanent relief, the reason I let him talk me into a one-on-one. By the time I reached the front door of the Hangover, I had weighed everything out. Better to endure one miserable discussion at a bar on the rough end of East Bay in which a final agreement would be reached than suffer worse aggravation, ongoing and never ending, at the hands of Stuart and Giselle. Which would surely be my fate if I bailed out before the meeting ever got started. No more being hammered with wave upon impassioned wave of drama-laced, emotion-soaked, woe-saturated requests for extended visitation from Stuart and the queen-of-pink. I had to put a final stop to it.

My original hope had been to solve the problem in a short discussion on the cottage back steps while Giselle waited in the yellow Mercedes. But Stuart, the most unhelpful man I have ever met, muffed that opportunity. I thought to give him two minutes to make one last plea to which I would respond with an arbitrary and resounding no. He, however, thought to forge a new beginning, a new future. He had always had a sixth sense about areas of my vulnerability, and this time was no different. And yet I was not at his complete mercy, not in the manner he believed. I was at the mercy of my own selfish desires.

I had no real understanding of the extent of my susceptibility that fateful day. Walking through the doorway of the Hangover Club was tantamount to walking through a looking glass. When the entrance fell away behind me, I did not realize I had just passed through the gates of hell. I forgot that Stuart was the same old wily serpent he had always been, never saying what he meant, never meaning what he said, forevermore concealing his wicked motives and hidden agendas. In my years apart from him, I had grown to value the straightforward. I'd worked diligently at becoming a genuine person in the hope it would make me a better mother. And the surprise was that I had made good progress. My life had gone from murky to transparent, at least in the upper stratums. What other reason would I have had for letting Stuart know about the twins in the first place than my determination to do the right thing. No more duality, not even when dealing with Stuart, the one person (except for my dysfunctional parents and heartless aunt) who had hurt me more than anyone else ever could. I wanted Raven and Constantia to know their father. Never mind I still had troubling questions about his involvement in Miss Peregrine's death. And if the presence of Stuart in the girls' lives meant I had to put up with Giselle, the living definition of pretense, then so be it. Now I ask you, could I have found a more honorable attitude to embrace? (I do wish you would stop smirking right to my face. It throws me off track in my narrative.)

So why then, given the loftiness of my new way of thinking, did I let Stuart lure me back into muddy waters? I am certain he thought mud was still my natural habitat, the question being was he right? Was my excursion into the clear stream of transparency a mere side trip, my new-found decency a sham? (Don't answer those questions, please. I am not able to deal with plain truth just yet, not after committing...well, you know my awful crime.)

13

After a good deal of stoking, I walked into the Hangover at three sharp according to the bells of St. Michael. My eyes adjusted slowly to the dim lighting the owner had been forced to install to camouflage the floor's inch-deep dust. I spied the urbane Stuart (not), the establishment's only customer, hunched over the bar from a tall stool. He looked like a classic case of idle day-drinking. Indeed, he did not just look the part, he was the part, lolling away his time on cheap alcohol, staring into space, thinking banal thoughts. I wondered how long he had been growing roots in that same spot and for how many apple-tinis.

I summoned my resolve, stiffened my shoulders, and walked across the room with counterfeit confidence. I felt the need to engage in a bit of swagger to subdue the case of angst I had been trying to quell since our stand-off in the driveway. In retrospect I admit the quiver in my stomach did not come from anxiety about saying no one more time to Stuart's requests for more visitation, but from raging guilt I felt in my gut from wishing I could shout yes.

For here was the ugly truth: More and more of late, deep within my most self-absorbed thoughts, I found myself toying with the notion of what a relief it would be to let him have his way. I imagined a scene in which I permitted Stuart and Giselle to beat me down with their relentless psychological warfare – all by my own design, of course – and force me to be more generous with Raven and Constantia's time. I would picture myself giving in to the argument that a lengthy visit might be good for everyone. Sometimes at night when I was tired, I enjoyed allowing this questionable little fantasy to play out in my mind, a controlled visualization in which, to Stuart's joy, I did not take offense when he presented his and Giselle's case for the hundredth time. Lately, even in the clarity of daylight, his requests had begun sounding more reasonable, even doable. It was becoming less difficult to kick Tycie's dire warnings out of the left hemisphere of my brain. What did an old woman know about visitation? Why not try a different approach? A month or so of extra time. See how things would progress. And if they went well, then proceed week-to-week as long as a comfort zone could be maintained for all.

Oh, dear. I did not mean to say comfort zone for all. I meant to say comfort zone for Raven and Constantia. (Really, it isn't necessary for you to bring that old shyster, Sigmond Freud, and his ideas about basic human selfishness into the mix right now. I know all about him and his theories.)

It was wrong to let my egocentric fantasies come to fruition, but degree by tiny degree my reprehensible self began getting it over on my newly principled self. No, no, I never went so far as to stop casting myself as the victim, and Stuart and Giselle as the villains. Which they were of the most revolting sort. But did their shortcomings make me superior? I think not. After all, I was the one who initially set the deadly events in motion. It still sickens me to recall how those events played out. Could the worst have been avoided by more sensible behavior on my part? I used to fret about this possibility every moment of every day, but due to the necessity of establishing sufficient equilibrium in the here-and-now to take proper care of my children, I had to stop worrying about what might have been. Confronting one's demons is an arduous endeavor. It is much easier to let them tend to their loathsome intrigues in the background unencumbered and unseen. What good is the stunning awareness they exist at all as they roam about invisibly in the realm of the air searching for souls to devour? Why not just ignore them?

Now you have met the real me, I suppose, that same old subtle creature of duality who has spent her life seeking purity of heart, but who remains a fractured mess. (Let me say right here, right now in the middle of my story, how frightfully nice it is to make your acquaintance. Let's have coffee sometime. Though you must be careful in my presence, for things are not always what they seem with me and certainly not what you would expect. But I digress. Let's pick up the pace of our journey. We have a shooting to attend, do we not?)

I recognize now I was the one who controlled the meeting at the Hangover, precision of hindsight being twenty-twenty. When I saw that Stuart was already in an alcohol fog, I decided to seize the moment. I went along with his need to convince me how desperately I needed a few weeks of freedom from the responsibility of parenting. And as he grew more and more fond of center stage, I allowed him to believe I was coming around to his way of thinking in response to his shining eloquence.

"Don't forget, Arlena," he said several times, earnest of expression, bleary of eyes. "You're this close to finishing your requirements for certification." On the word, this, he snapped his fingers, which made me blink. "You've got nothing left but student teaching, which, by the way, could sink your entire effort if you blow it. What are you planning to do about child care? Mrs. Lupio is old. You can't expect her to watch the girls day and night."

I let him go on for a long while, stacking up his brilliant points, virtue signaling like some politician from hell. I admit it was irritating to hear him express interest in my personal needs when it was obvious he thought them mundane. The weird thing was that I agreed. My personal needs were definitely mundane. Problems relative to childcare were routine for any working mom, not just me, and not insurmountable. Why did I let Stuart believe he had convinced me I deserved special consideration? The uncomfortable answer to that question boiled down to one big rotten egg with a bad odor. Yes, Stuart and Giselle committed sins all right, but they were not alone. I surpassed them in malevolence in the end, the reason my conscience will not let me rest. For my guilt is not limited to remorse over killing another human being. I now must live with the disturbing knowledge that some evil behaviors can be more subtle than simple murder...and far more destructive.

14

I took a seat on the bar stool next to Stuart and asked the bartender for water with no ice. Stuart fumbled around making room for me, standing up, sitting down, adjusting his own stool, until I told him if he did not stop, I was going to run out of there screaming.

"What would you like?" he said. "Beer? A spritzer?"

"I already ordered water."

"Oh, yeah, sorry. Guess I'm jumpy from bringing Giselle up here from Florida. Believe me, she doesn't get Charleston."

He paused and fiddled with his drink stirrer, took a false sip, droned on. "She doesn't get you, either, not when it comes to Raven and Constantia. You intimidate her. That's why she comes across like she's talking down. Not that you aren't talking down too. You are...on purpose. Must be a woman thing." He paused and stared into his capri martini glass for an answer to the meaning of life. "It was a mistake to bring her here."

I stopped him. I was tired of his sloppy drunk act. "Yes, a huge mistake, but nothing else would do, would it? Insecure Giselle couldn't stand the thought of her irresistible new hubby coming to Charleston alone to meet with his drop-dead-gorgeous ex-wife. You don't have to explain the situation. Her feelings aren't uncommon. We do have a history, you and I...married once-upon-a-time, children, divorced. Giselle has a valid point of view. It's just... well...she's such a dope. Oops, sorry I said that. Oops, no, I'm not."

Stuart took several real sips of his martini while I continued elevating myself at Giselle's expense. He was certain the part I threw in about her having a valid point of view was lip-service. And from the look on the bartender's face, he was pretty sure as well.

Stuart remained quiet long enough to give me an edge. I was beginning to like the sound of my own voice, until Stu got tired of my ridiculousness and began talking over me.

"No matter what I tell her, Arly, no matter how much she sees us fighting over Raven and Constantia, she's still afraid we have feelings for each other. Not that it's important to her, nothing thousands of dineros in shopping can't cure. That's where she went when she dropped me off here, shopping. By now, she's had half the antiques on King Street shipped to Massachusetts and the other half to Florida. We're flying to Boston in a few days to help her parents get organized to move into their Winter Park condo. Which means Giselle and I will be hanging out in their main house on Lake Osceola in town. She told me last night her parents like living in a smaller place now that they're getting older. Lucky for us...frees up the villa. Isn't it great Winter Park is so close to Orlando? Raven and Constantia love Mickey and Minnie."

I glanced at the mirror behind the shelves of liquor bottles. Was that steam shooting out of my ears? "For the record, Stuart, you nouveau-riche-wannabe, I don't care where you and Giselle hang out. And as for Mickey and Minnie, Raven and Constantia think they eat hot fudge sundaes for lunch every day like you let them do. Don't you and Giselle ever think of anything to fill your time other than commercial entertainment? Everybody knows Disney is a ker-ching machine."

Stuart formed an oval with his lips and blew out a noisy sigh. "Sheeze, Arlena. The older you get, the more hostile. I don't know why Giselle would ever think I still care. Maybe it's a function programmed into women's brains. Ex-wife... natural enemy to current wife...hate required from both directions. Giselle may be trapped in the only lane available to her."

I held up my water glass and studied the greasy fingerprints on its side. "Is she or isn't she?" I said. "I for one do not care."

"Arly, please, don't...not when I'm depressed like this. Look around. It's a nice afternoon. I could get into asking you to love me again. After three martinis, I start thinking about ditching Giselle and her dough. I miss you. I miss the girls."

"Ditching Giselle and her dough?" I said. "Not her looks, her kind heart? It's her checkbook you couldn't bear to lose. Martinis have always been truth serum for you, Stuart. Have another."

"You're not being fair. All I want is what I've never had...Raven and Constantia. Let them come with me...for a little while. I need them."

The muscles in my face arranged themselves into a look of sarcasm, the same old default mode I had been trying to suppress for years. Stuart read it with accuracy and resorted to his own default, arguing back at me like a mad man, loud, overbearing. "What kind of woman comes between children and their father?"

I had been wondering where the real Stuart was hiding. It was kind of good to have him back. Kind of real. His sudden testosterone rant caused the bartender to drop a stack of cocktail napkins to the C-rated-for-filthiness rubber mats behind the bar. They landed in a fan at his feet, but instead of recovering them, he got involved in a different task, rearranging his massive collection of beer steins that were greasier with fingerprints than my water glass.

I paid no attention to what the bartender was doing. I was interested in the fact the Stuart I knew best had reared his disagreeable head. And though I had encountered this Stuart many times in the past and knew all about his feet of clay, he still had the power to offend. "You're killing me," he said with venom. "You really are."

Now that was an appalling figure of speech, another omen, if you will. Stuart had no clue how close he'd come to predicting his own fate. He would have bolted if he had. But being Stuart, he kept on talking. "I'm sick of you power-tripping on me. You've been doing it since Raven and Connie were born. Cheated me out of their first two years altogether. They were already walking and talking the first time I laid eyes on them. And now they're four, and I see them, what? Six or seven times a year for short weekends? Most men would have done something legal about it a long time ago, hauled you into court. And you know very well why I haven't. At first, before Giselle, I thought you and I might have a shot at being a couple again, that you might love me again. It's the reason I waited so long to get married. I wanted to be with you, Arlena… you and Raven and Connie. Heaven, help me…sometimes I still do."

The bartender took a break from rearranging his beer steins to curse me with his best hate stare. I cursed him right back with a savage stare of my own, then I continued power-tripping on Stuart, a curious phrase that sounded more like an electrical problem than a character flaw. Did Stuart really teach English at the college level in the past? Or was that a lie too?

I said in my best power-tripping tone, "Her name is Constantia, not Connie…you poser." It felt so good beating on Stuart that I decided to beat on him some more. "Connie is my pet name for my baby, and I won't allow it to be bandied about by the likes of you and what's-her-face. And don't get any funny ides about separating the girls. Just because they're twins doesn't mean one there's for you and one for me. They're both mine. You've never paid a dime of child support, but somehow you don't see a disconnect between that and spewing out cheap talk about wanting to love me again, sending me sappy poetry, twilight-and-memory-and-towers-in-the sky. I know it's all dreams and alcohol. You never showed any serious interest in Raven and Constantia until Giselle found out she couldn't get pregnant. I'm their mother, their only mother, and the two of you aren't taking them away from me. Let Giselle buy herself some other children like she buys everything else…houses, cars, husbands. How long has it been since you worked anywhere?"

Stuart rose from the bar stool, stepped into my personal space, and said with a scary growl, "As if you aren't into Miss Peregrine's dough. Don't think I haven't wised up to that. You got way more than that piddly lump sum check you split with me."

He stood over me six inches, exhaling the venom of alcohol rage. I tried not to let him see me cower as he shouted louder. "As far as I've seen, Miss Better-Than-Everybody-Else, you haven't done a thing Miss Peregrine asked you to in that bizarre will of hers…unless there was a paragraph I missed about working the cash register at a beach dive on Isle of Palms. What's the name of it? One-Eyed Parrot? Sell a few margaritas, serve some free trail-mix, chat up a few drunks? And the next morning, dump your children off at whatever childcare you can scrape up so you can go back to acting like a co-ed again at The Citadel of all places, a military school if you haven't noticed. Yep, Raven and Constantia have told me about your motherly habits."

"Two weeks," I said. For some reason my voice had turned squeaky. "I worked at the Parrot two lousy weeks when the owners – my friends from Sullivan's, by the way – were desperate for help during the tourist season. It was a favor. No pay. And don't ever come at me again for taking graduate courses. I want to live a productive life. Mr. Pinckney takes care of Miss Peregrine's estate. And he's grooming his grandson to take over when he's old enough. It won't ever be my life's work. I'm trying to get a degree useful to humanity, unlike your lame PhD in English, good for nothing but teaching 101 and 102 in tier-C colleges. I want to work in a public school, not throw my life away for the sake of stupid status like you've always done, running around chasing I-don't-know-what."

Stuart got a peculiar look on his face and backed off. It was as if for a milli-second he saw through my façade. On thinking back, I'm sure he did. He dialed down the volume of his voice, though I did not trust this as a positive. No matter how serious he forced himself to be, I noticed the skin over his cheekbones remained inflamed. "Look," he said with nervous calm. "You might not believe me, but I admire you for going back to school. It was a cool move."

He was right. I did not believe that lie nor the next ten. "Arlena, I know you're doing the best you can for the girls, but you're human, not a super hero. It's difficult being a mom and going to school at the same time. You need help, the kind of help Giselle and I can give you. Let us keep the girls…just while you do your student teaching. Why not? It'll be good for everybody. Raven and Constantia will have fun. You can focus on your work. And Giselle and I will be forever grateful for the extra time. And after you finish, you can find yourself a do-gooder job in some do-gooder school and get back to being the best mom in the world. I'm offering you an opportunity here. Relax, take a little help."

Tycie's warning echoed in my head like a chancel bell. Was she hiding in a shadowy corner of the bar? Had she slipped in without my seeing her? I shuddered and wiped away the perspiration now beading on my forehead. Then I shut the narrow door to Tycie's wisdom and opened the wide gate to folly.

Now then...let us – you and I – stop for a moment and regroup. I want to make sure you don't think I'm still playing at self-deception. I did not – I repeat, did not – believe for one second that Stuart felt empathy for me. And yet I plowed forward pretending to believe that particular lie simply because I wanted to so much. The strange thing was, though I needed no pretense at all to fool Stuart, I required massive amounts to fool myself. Oh, yes, I was more than able to hear the overtones of deceit in my speech as I responded to his last, most cunning suggestion. The timbre of my voice went high-pitched and shrill, my gabble disgusting and girlish. "Oh, Stu, do you really think it would be okay for me to do it that way even if my heart is saying no? Do you think? Do you?"

Stuart smiled victory. He had already realized the no I had been proclaiming for nearly an hour in the dirty shadows of the Hangover Club was different from all the others. This no meant yes.

15

"Guess what. I got a job."

Reynolds Lucinda Brentwood – my red-haired friend, Rennie – burst into the cottage with her usual high spirits, ignoring as she had since her arrival to Charleston from Texas that I was working at my computer. "Rennie," I said without looking away from the screen, "your husband owns three oil wells. Your father-in-law's birthday gift to your mother-in-law was an east Texas petroleum field. What do you need with a job?"

"I'm not talking about things like that around here, and don't you, either. I can't get away from it back home."

"Then maybe you should take those three-caret studs out of your ears. Someone may catch on. You aren't slumming it here in Charleston, you know. Locals can spot the real thing."

Rennie flopped down on the sofa and kicked off her Jimmy Choo flats. I still wasn't looking at her directly, yet it was impossible to miss that her toes were sporting a trendy new gel color… Strawberries-in-July. At least that's what my long-term house guest (dear Rennie herself) had announced earlier in the day to the au naturel, plain-toed me.

My old pal propped her feet on the coffee table for ease in admiring her own pedi. She wiggled her short fat toes and laughed aloud at their cuteness, effectively destroying the last shred of my concentration. "My feelings are hurt," she said, a declaration nowhere near the truth. "You didn't ask a single question about my new job. Just for that, I'm not going to try to get you on the payroll too."

"Like I could handle moonlighting on top of student teaching. But enough about me. Let's talk about you. Or better still, let's talk about your unsuspecting employer's new stress level, the one he doesn't know he has yet."

"I don't cause people stress. Jimmy Buffet over at the One-Eyed Parrot loved me in my interview."

"What?" My eyes no longer focused on the computer monitor, but on my friend's face. "Why did you go over there, Rennie? You found out I'm friends with the owner, didn't you? What did you tell Pete?"

"You aren't friends with Pete. You don't have friends. Acquaintances, maybe, but no friends. And I didn't say a thing, only that you and I go way back and you'll be calling him sometime today to give me a stellar recommendation. I can see why you like cozying up over there. The tiki bar alone would make Ernest Hemingway a happy man. Pete is starting me out on the late shift. Not full time, though. Three nights a week. Their regular girl from Awendaw is pregnant with triplets. Don't look so horrified. Working at a bar will be fun. I'll meet a few people, make the most of my short visit. You were so miserly to limit me to one semester when you knew I wanted to squat here forever."

I studied Rennie's smiling eyes and plump cheeks which were as full of life as her springy red curls. I had not been able to decipher the real reason she was camping out in the cottage with me. It was not to finish her degree as she pretended. She could have done that back home in Dallas. I was starting to think it was as simple as the adventure factor, the need to escape dull routine. Not that it made any difference. I didn't care what her reasons were. My role was to provide her sanctuary and a temporary dwelling place, not be let in on the whole truth. And while Raven and Constantia were in Florida with Stuart during my student teaching block, I was thankful for her company. There would be little room for sad-and-lonely with Rennie Brentwood in the house.

I knew I was in for the unexpected while she was there, but not the roller coaster ride she presented. A more intuitive soul than I would have felt more in the way of foreboding. On reflection, I think I did. But I was so good at ignoring the obvious that quicksand on the path right in front of me would have eluded my attention. I believed in the mirage that I had a workable plan (you do not have to point out how delusional this was), the most important component of which was allowing Stuart to take Raven and Constantia off my hands the few short weeks it would take me to finish my student teaching requirement. As for the troublesome wisps of intuition that floated in and out of my brain every day... mental alerts suggesting things may not be as peachy as they appeared on the surface...I shoved them back into the shadows. I coped by reminding myself that a neurotic fear of the future had always been and would always be a fixed trait in my personality, motherhood notwithstanding. It seemed better to concentrate on checking off tasks associated with student teaching than entertain thoughts of doom. I chose to disregard the persistent case of jitters that stole my appetite too often, plus the night sweats that interfered with my sleep. Again and again, I had to go back to the fact that existing under the pall of a general sense of dread was my normal and customary state.

Sometimes now I am able to forgive myself for discounting the many warnings that came my way. Sometimes, but not all the time. For example, I will never be able to come to grips with my choice to reject – outcome be damned – Tycie's advice about keeping Raven and Constantia close to me while they were little. I am glad you don't have to look back on your own life with such terrible regret...tongue firmly in cheek...for I know there are many times, most likely when the wee hours of morning are playing havoc with your sleep, that you contemplate with sheer horror every decision you have ever made.

16

My drive back from Columbia was exhausting. I had spent the whole day and part of the evening slaving away in the bowels of the University of South Carolina library, working on the literature review section of my last practicum. My inner voice told me it was a bad idea to start home after eight o'clock, but continuing along my usual oppositional track, I got on the road immediately. Which put my arrival at Sullivan's well past ten. Tired and hungry, I was glad for the lift in spirits I felt when the cottage came into view. Every window was aglow. Never in Rennie's sheltered life had she thought about the cost of electricity. For once, I considered this a plus. Her presence meant I did not have to return to a dark, empty house. Raven and Constantia's absence tore at me at times. I missed them every moment, but more so during evening hours, the reason I did not phone them when I left the library. I hadn't trusted my ability to keep my composure. No sense making little ones feel responsible for their mother's tears. Unfair is what that would be.

On reaching the safety of the cottage driveway, I slumped against the steering wheel and breathed a prayer of thanks for traveling mercies. Sore muscles and burning eyes were enough to endure. No way I could have dealt with a road incident. My prayer helped me gather enough strength for the trek across the driveway. Rennie's BMW, her high-dollar rental car, routinely took up so much space in the parking area that I was seldom able to maneuver my own vehicle between the pilings to park under the cottage. I missed the small luxury of the covered space, but had given it up without a fuss. On the few occasions I'd been able to access it, I had been blocked in and made late to wherever I needed to be, something not tolerated for student teacher hopefuls. On Rennie's arrival, unsheltered parking and weary treks to the front steps became my reality.

On this tired night, I did not bother to unload my school gear. I was barely able to manage my purse. Its strap cut into my shoulder as I tramped in slow motion toward the outdoor stairs. Exhaustion rendered the climb to the second floor longer and harder. On making it to the kitchen door, I found it locked tight. Sighing, I fumbled in my purse for the Explorer key ring, wishing I had not been so quick to drop it inside. The doorbell was not an option. Every light burning did not mean Rennie was up. But the second my fingers touched the keys, my quirky housemate tricked me by flinging open the door and welcoming me home with the biggest grin ever. I was instantly suspicious, a feeling that intensified when she offered to take my heavy purse off my hands.

"You're home," she chirped. Was that honest glee in her voice or had she done something? I strained to separate lies from truth as she chattered on. "I was about to send out the highway patrol. We need a better system for staying in touch. I don't like worrying where you are in the middle of the night in bad weather. Tomorrow, I'm getting you a better phone, one that actually holds a charge."

Though suspicious, I played along. "It's ten thirty, not the middle of the night, and the weather isn't bad out. You never worried about me when you were in Texas all those years."

She insisted on her concern as she tugged me inside. "I wasn't responsible for you then. My mother used to tell me she didn't worry about me one bit the whole time I was away at school, but let me come home for a break, and she couldn't sleep at night 'til she knew I was safe in my own bed. Anyway I've got a surprise. But be quiet, the surprise is sleeping."

And now the truth comes slithering out, I thought, congratulating myself on knowing it had been lurking beneath the surface all along. Anticipating the worst, I gave in to my friend pulling me toward the living room. When Reynolds Brentwood labeled something a surprise, it was time to get nervous. Unhappy memories of the pet rabbit she had kept in our dorm room for a month popped into my mind. She had rescued the poor thing after the psychology lab was finished letting freshmen torment it with behavior modification experiments. But tonight, the stray I saw sleeping on my sofa made me long for one as innocuous as Mr. Pink Nose.

I stared a moment at the sand-colored hair that hung in a long wavy curtain off the sofa seat. Hair was all I could see of the human form unconscious under my favorite blue afghan, the last one Tycie had knitted before her hands got too stiff with arthritis.

I said not a word, disengaged my hand from Rennie's, and walked straight into my own bedroom to begin the business of getting ready for bed. No way could I cope with Rapunzel until I had gotten some rest. But Rennie was not letting me off the hook so easily. She followed me, bumbling into my back at my closet door.

"Think of it as a ministry," she said.

A ministry? Was she kidding me? The whole cottage smelled like booze from Rapunzel's breath.

"Everyone needs help sometimes," she rattled on. "What's wrong with a friend crashing on your couch for the night? You know how harsh the law can be when it comes to public intoxication. Staying here would be better than risking jail, right?"

I pulled on a pair of leggings and a t-shirt and went about putting my hair up in a ponytail in preparation for sleep, all without defending myself or the privacy of my home, the integrity of which I was trying to preserve for my children. It was becoming apparent allowing Rennie to fly east and spend a couple of months (the opening statement of her discourse on how well she would behave if I would let her come) had been a huge mistake, one I had not figured out how to correct.

Okay, I thought to myself without speaking. Don't make rash decisions when you're tired and fuzzy-headed. Wait until the light of day. Morning has a way of making bad things look better.

Aloud, I said with as little irritation as I could muster, "Please, Rennie, let me go to bed. I can't handle…"

"Oh, no, no, no," she said. "I'm done with the silent treatment. Back in college, I tolerated that junky behavior of yours, but this is a new day. We're big girls now. I can do whatever I want without you squelching me out of habit. What exactly is the issue? I know you aren't selfish. You'd put up with Jack the Ripper if he were down on his luck. I'm here, aren't I?"

I stopped in the middle of hanging up my skirt and looked at her, the beautiful, bosomy Rennie, whose clothes and makeup were far too suggestive for a woman her age. Giving up on my wish for a smooth transition from travel to rest, I inhaled an extra half-liter of oxygen and addressed the root problem. "Perhaps," I said, "we should have established a few ground rules at the start. I thought you had grown up, learned some judgment. You know… changed."

"Me? What about you? You haven't changed a lick. Financial security, two fabulous children, nothing has lifted the black cloud you've been slogging around under your whole life. You haven't smiled twice since I've been here. I told myself it was because the kids were with Stuart. But that's not it. You're the same weirdo you were back in college. And what's worse, you like it. You cultivate it."

"Look, Rennie. We're two grown women set in our ways. Even you know we can't have another woman in the house without complications. I realize how big your heart is, bigger than Texas. And tomorrow morning, after your new friend in there tells you the rest of her hard-luck story, you'll want to adopt her and move her in to raise. I'm not going to say that doesn't make me mad, 'cause it does. It makes me furious. You can't invite a woman to crash in another woman's house without asking permission."

I waited for Rennie's objections, fully expecting her to throw a big bucket of Texas crude oil onto the bonfire I had just lit. But she did not. She did the opposite. I watched, confused, as a half-smile formed on her lips, effectively ending our fight before it got off to a good start. The determined Rennie marched back into the living room and returned within seconds, her foundling at her side. I stared at the two of them standing before me. For the foundling was not a woman, but a man, an astonishingly young and good-looking man. Whose height I was unable to judge as he was leaning so heavily upon Rennie. Not that his height mattered. His distinguishing feature was his hair, a luxurious mane that draped across Rennie's torso. He was a stunner all right, even under the influence of alcohol – eyes closed, face serene, body relaxed.

The silence in the room lengthened as I looked him up and down. And then, unable to help myself, I burst out laughing. And Rennie laughed with me until she began swaying under Peter Pan's weight. I rushed forward and grabbed his free arm, and together Rennie and I guided him back to the sofa and helped him get prone again. He never once opened his eyes, never spoke, never acknowledged Rennie or me. Just cuddled up with Constantia's Mickey Mouse pillow and began snoring like a child.

"Drunk as a bandicoot," Rennie said as she tucked the blanket around him. "Came in the restaurant tonight and bellied up to the bar, drank five vodka tonics in an hour. He was doing okay, not causing a ruckus or anything, but then he started talking too loud. Came around the bar and got down on his knees in front of me and begged me to marry him and have his children. Pete wanted to call the police and have him picked up, but I said I knew him and would give him a ride home. I'd worked the early shift for Pete on account of his bar tender from Mt. Pleasant can't keep her anti-depressant meds regulated."

I interrupted Rennie's fairy tale with reality. "You cannot bring home every kid who drinks too much at the Parrot. We aren't running a shelter here. And it's dangerous. I mean, he's cute and all, but he could be a serial killer."

"No, no. I wasn't lying. I do know him. He's the model for my drawing class. He poses nude two hours on Thursdays and Fridays. Now that's a sight to see. Our prof announced yesterday it's the only time in the history of his thirty-year career that not a single person has cut class. One of the townies is a senior citizen. Old people get to audit classes free paid for by the state. This lady, ninety if she's a day, drags her stool within three feet of him every class and sketches different parts of his anatomy. Everyone says she's getting it all to perfection so she can put the pieces together later like a puzzle…make a life-size portrait to glue to the ceiling above her bed."

I backed up to an easy chair and dropped into it. Rennie went on talking. Sleeping Beauty went on snoring. I went on considering what new madness had come my way.

"I promise you, Arly. I do know him sort of. We've been for coffee twice. He's a nice kid, struggling to get through undergraduate school on no money, and, I might add, not as young as he looks. Says he's twenty-seven, but I don't believe it. Probably not more than twenty-one or two."

"And why would he lie about his age? Most people want you to think they're younger, not older."

"A younger man will always fudge higher when he's trying to date an older woman. They all do it."

"And how do you know so much? You've been married since you left college. Most women give up dating when they get married."

"Guys under twenty-five don't count. They're playmates. They can dance and stay up late and show you their muscles. That's not dating. That's frolicking."

"Frolicking?" I said, eyeing the immobile figure on the sofa. "This dude can't even walk by himself."

"Well, they are immature. You have to put them to bed and make them get their rest and things like that, or they'll overdo and get sick. That's what happened to Hal last night. Hal is his first name. I can't think of his last. Anyway, he overdid majorly. His parents phoned him yesterday and told him his dad had lost his job – the company he worked for downsized or something – and they have to stop sending him money for school. Things were tight as they were. And now he's three weeks into the semester with no cash. Can't buy food, can't pay his half of apartment expenses. I don't know why a little thing like no rent money got his roommate so upset. Something about they'd put down a non-refundable deposit on the apartment. It's in the attic of one of those old monster houses in the historic district downtown. People in Charleston love to rent out rat holes to outsiders, don't they? More like the pre-historic district. Anyhoo, Hal decided the sensible thing to do given the circumstances was to get himself to a beach bar and drown his troubles in drink, so he came out to see little-ole-me at the Parrot and spent the last of his money on booze."

"He has a car? How can he afford a car if he's broke?"

"Hitch-hiked. I almost died when he told me. He's too much of a pretty-boy to be hitching. Some kook could get ideas."

"He can't stay here, Rennie." Silent pause. "You know that, right?"

She sighed. "Don't worry. He'll leave when he wakes up. I'll drive him back to town in the morning and drop him off at his apartment. Maybe the cranky old roommate will have settled down by then."

For an unclear moment, I thought Rennie was talking about me, the cranky old roommate. Then I realized she was talking about some poor schmuck two bridges away who from the sound of things was in worse shape tenant-wise than I.

17

Two weeks later, Hal – Hal Morris, to be exact – had not missed a night of peaceful slumber upon my living room sofa, nor a daytime commute to school in Rennie's rented vehicle...with her driving. During their honeymoon of sorts, Rennie had gotten him a job bussing tables at the Parrot the same three nights she was on the schedule, helped him with his homework every day, washed and dried his threadbare clothes, and bought him a new pair of flip-flops.

I did not complain when he moved from the sofa to her bedroom, or when he slipped into the routine of making coffee and toast for the three of us every morning, or started washing the dishes and mopping the kitchen and vacuuming the house. In private conversations with myself, I came to the inaccurate conclusion that throwing him out would be unproductive, indeed, would accomplish nothing beyond turning Rennie into sad sack of the year. So...since the entire living arrangement was temporary, I elected to put up with Rennie's boy-toy for the time being. It was a bad decision devoid of wise analysis, but it was the easiest way out which was all I wanted at the time. I knew Dallas was Rennie's touchstone. And when she got tired of Prince Hal and me, off to D-Town she would skip-a-fandango without a thought about either one of us. Which would be the end of her odd new ministry.

Besides, I was too busy with school to squander my strength on nonsense. And though Rennie was not quiet by any definition, Hal was the ultimate silent type. He seldom made noise of any kind and never caused trouble unless you want to label staring trouble. He stared a great deal which made me uncomfortable. I said as much to Rennie one night while he was in the shower, who informed me he had made the same observation about me. Quoting him, she said, "Why is your friend so somber, and why does she dislike me so much?"

Since I've always thought he-said/she-said tiresome, I shared no other thoughts about Hal with Rennie, and no other criticism. If she wanted to fantasize it was A-OK for a married woman like herself to consort with a male undergraduate, and that he was a swell guy and she was a swell girl, it would have to remain between the two of them. I had no time to sit in judgment. Nothing was more important to me than finishing my student teaching obligation and getting Raven and Constantia back home.

Rennie took advantage of my distraction. While I went on with real life, she and Hal went on with make-believe. And what, you might ask, was her oil baron husband doing with his time back in the Lone Star State? Your guess is as good as mine. But whatever it was, Rennie was not interested. Why then should it concern you or me?

Student teaching was not my only knotty problem. Difficulties relative to my studies cropped up daily. True, student teaching made for rough going, but other things, like my final practicum, also added stress. I had no time to bother with my housemates' issues. I had enough of my own.

Which brings me to a basic question: Why did I want a teaching credential at all? Even now I have trouble unpacking my subconscious reasons for becoming obsessed with such a goal. Was it a function of the same old compulsion I have suffered from all my life? The need to set goals and objectives, put pressure on myself and pile up accomplishments, all to prove myself worthy? Or maybe I harbored a certain resentment toward Stuart for expecting me to sacrifice my own schooling to work and support him while he finished his. Why had not I turned the whole concept around, required Stuart to waste his own time on menial jobs while I pursued an advanced degree? You are right. The answer is obvious. I was a victim of social and cultural norms of the time. I wonder, were you a victim as well?

But enough about the distant past. Let's move forward to the time right before a single gunshot split the world apart. Those were the days I studied nonstop while Rennie and Hal played...also nonstop. I offer no explanation of their type of play. You will have to use your imagination. My own work, however, I can pontificate upon until you turn blue in the face and fall over. The most onerous assignment weighing me down, in addition to student teaching, was the practicum I mentioned earlier. It was not an arduous project, just cumbersome in that it required several trips to USC's Cooper Library in Columbia in the name of research. For reasons I was not able to fathom at the time, my advisor at The Citadel was seeing to it that I searched primary sources housed deep in the rare book section of dusty old Cooper Library. I did not realize until almost finished with the work that I was actually conducting research for the advisor himself. Way later, when I glanced at an article he had published proudly in a national education journal, I marveled at how familiar I was with every source cited in his bibliography. Welcome to the sly world of academia.

But my discovery at how shamelessly the professor was using me compared in no way to the shenanigans going on in my own household. In retrospect, I am shocked by the antics I endured. Subliminally I must have realized danger was about. This realization, methinks, was the reason I did not resist more when Rennie called and asked to come stay with me for a short visit. Though I professed otherwise, I was glad to have her around. I, the consummate loner, did not want to be alone. Working to exhaustion was not enough to stop me from second-guessing my decision to let Raven and Constantia go with Stuart. I fretted often and desperately about his and Giselle's extreme efforts to bond with my children, crazy-making thoughts from which I needed respite. Enter Rennie. Enter more than respite. Enter a whirling dervish.

For Rennie did not come to Charleston to take care of me or anyone else, including herself. It became clear within minutes of her arrival that her intention was to extract as many razzle-dazzle moments as she could from her interlude in the Holy City. Which explains how and why she got around to Hal so quickly. His presence in the cottage helped her put reality on the run until the novelty of his hair and physique wore off and boredom set in again. In college, her favorite strategy for eradicating monotony was to throw money at it. I'd hoped married life had tempered this pattern, but on a Friday night at the end of one of my manic weeks of schoolwork, I discovered it had not.

"Pack your week-end bags before bed, you indulged children," she said to Hal and me over an outdoor sunset dinner of peel-and-eat shrimp and red rice. My lame idea that we were okay-with-chardonnay blew away in a puff of Rennie's vaping steam. She had something more expensive in mind for entertainment.

"We're going on a jaunt," she said. "Aren't the two of you so blessed to have me for a friend?"

I have no idea what was going on in Hal's head at the time, but I for one hoped Rennie was talking about a quick trip to Central Florida. We had done that once before, driven to Winter Park in the Explorer, picked up the girls from Stuart and Giselle, checked in at the Wilderness Lodge on the Disney property for a single night (Rennie could afford anything), and spent a few hours in the Magic Kingdom before dark. After which, Rennie and Hal took the shuttle to Pleasure Island to bar hop along the neon strip... without me, of course. All I wanted was to soak up every moment with my children before having to say goodbye again on Sunday.

But that had been less than two weeks past and against Stuart's will. I knew he would freak if I showed up again so soon. Still...

"Winter Park?" I said expectantly to the mischievous Rennie.

"No, no, and no. Stop being such a boring mom. This trip is for grownups. Raven and Constantia are fine where they are, happy as fairies. We're going to the Big Apple, and it's my jazzy treat."

And we did...and had a good time...at first. Rennie saw to it with her wallet. The Algonquin Hotel, dinner at Bella Vita's, drinks at the Marquis rooftop revolving bar. I did not recognize myself. Had a new woman taken up residence in my old skin? With Rennie in the lead, one felt like part of a celebrity entourage, great fun for a while. But it did not last. As always with Rennie, there was the required veering off course.

After dragging ourselves back to our hotel late Saturday night, I decided to take a shower before tucking in. Afterward, when my alcohol head refused to stop aching, I knocked on the connecting door to Rennie and Hal's room to ask if they had any aspirin. Whereupon, Rennie cracked the door and stared at me with dull eyes. I apologized for waking her, but then I caught a familiar odor drifting through the doorway.

"What are you doing in there?" I said. "Do you have weed? Where did you get weed in the city?"

"It's not mine. It's Hal's. He brought it with him. And it's really good. Want some?"

She opened the door wider and invited me into their room with a silly gesture. I took a step back. Rennie bent over double laughing, though I saw nothing funny. It was her marijuana laugh. I knew it. I had heard it before. "Come in," she said, still chuckling at my consternation. "It's great stuff. Hal says he's never had better."

"What if someone calls security, Rennie? You can smell things through the vents. Is that someone coming already, from down the hallway?"

My whole body began trembling with rage and fury. I was about to say more, but Rennie snatched me into her and Hal's room and demanded I stop talking so loudly. She ran and grabbed a mash-up of smoking paraphernalia off a table by the window, stuffed everything into a tote, and hid it in her carry-on case. Then she took the small bag of marijuana into the bathroom, and in seconds, I heard the toilet flush.

By this time, Hal had scrambled to his feet and was standing with his back pressed against a wall. He was shallow of breath, wild of eye, stricken with terror, the consummate poster boy for paranoia - Pot Is the Gateway to Psychosis. Just say no!"

I judged him harshly in my mind, never stopping to think that in the very near future, I myself would commit a crime far worse than smoking a raggedy joint in a hotel room. I judged Rennie, too, who, on emerging empty-handed from the bathroom began a pompous speech insisting that the person who had paid the tab for the whole weekend should be allowed to do whatever she pleased, and I (me) had no right to spoil her fun.

Rennie usually needed two joints and three cocktails to make her that self-righteous. I needed nothing at all, not even a root beer. I was born the corrupt judge of everyone's character except my own. I countered Rennie's disorganized tirade with my own harangue about how I'd hoped she had grown up since college, and that I could not believe she cared nothing at all about putting me at risk of losing custody of my children. I lowered my voice when I asked her if she and Hal had any more MJ back at the cottage. "Has it occurred to you," I said in haughty conclusion, "what Stuart could do to me with a thing like that?"

Rennie took the floor again and declared I wasn't superior, and she was sick-and-tired of bowing and scraping before my rotten disposition. She finished with a flourish of name-calling. Said she, "Go back to your own room, you holier-than-thou, moralistic, buzz kill. Leave Hal and me alone."

I refused to obey either command, not until the name-caller herself had assured me, even if lying through her ultra-whitened teeth, that no MJ whatsoever was in the cottage. "Rennie, listen to me. I can't risk losing my children over something as asinine as pot."

She softened then and said she hadn't thought about it in that light, but not to worry, there was nothing back in the cottage and for me to relax and go to bed. She promised they had brought along only a few ounces, just enough to have a little fun on the trip, and that was all there was, and there wasn't any more, and I was making a big fuss over nothing.

I did not ask where they had acquired their few ounces, nor mention the cold feeling that ran through me at the thought of airport officials finding MJ in their luggage. I just went back to my own room with no aspirin and lay awake the rest of the night.

My headache turned into a marathon migraine with accompanying nausea that did not ease off until dawn. By six thirty, the actual pain was gone, but had left in its wake a familiar soreness to the brain and scalp. If you suffer from migraines, you know what I am talking about. If you don't, get down on your knees and give thanks.

When my phone alarm went off at seven, I groped for it on the bedside table to shut if off before my head blew up again. I knew from experience that silence helps counter the after-effects of a migraine. Too bad Rennie and Hal also heard the alarm. They rapped on the connecting door at five after seven, and when I did not answer, both slunk into my room uninvited.

Apologies and contrition abounded. They thought I was still angry, but I was not. I was silent out of fear the headache would return. My skull still felt encased in a steel band. Rennie interpreted my unwillingness to talk as the cold shoulder. She watched as I moved slowly around the room getting my belongings together for the flight home; insisted she didn't blame me for not speaking to her; apologized for everything again and again; admitted bringing the marijuana was her idea, not Hal's; told me how sorry she was to have done something so stupid; owned up to the seriousness of it relative to the welfare of Raven and Constantia; said she and Hal would understand if I threw them out of the cottage the minute we got back to Charleston; and finished up with an earnest pledge that if I'd let them stay and finish out the semester, they would not do anything like that ever again.

Almost in a whisper, I said, "Were you telling the truth about pot in the cottage?"

"No, no, no," she said. "I mean…yes, yes, yes. We brought all we had with us. I swear it on the life of Betsy Ross."

"Betsy Ross is your goldfish, Rennie." I paused to think, an extraordinarily difficult thing to attempt in the wake of a migraine. "All right," I said. "Don't mention this to me again, particularly the part about transporting anything questionable across state lines on a plane. My children…"

Rennie teared up. "You're right," she said. "Like always, you're right. But nobody's perfect. You, either. Remember that time in college when you…"

"Enough," I said. "I know who I used to be. But what we have to do now is go back home and finish what we started with our schoolwork. As for him," I gestured toward Hal, "from this day forward, he's your problem, not mine. I'm done with him."

"Are you saying we can stay 'til the end of term? Oh, thank you, Arly, thank you, thank you."

Her lips twitched with desire to say more, but she forced herself not to, for which I was thankful. Her theatrical apology had seemed almost genuine, though it was not the reason I forgave her. I am sure you think I'm going to try to convince you I forgave her out of friendship. Though you and I both know the real reason. I could not face staying in the cottage alone, not while Raven and Constantia were still with Stuart.

Experience informed me the new advantage I had managed to get over Rennie would not last long. Therefore, I milked the moment by requiring her and Hal to swear, separately and together, that marijuana as a form of recreation was over in my children's home. Rennie put on her best guilty-dog look and made Hal do the same. Speaking for the two of them, she repeated with exaggerated emotion how grateful they were for being allowed to continue on in the cottage. She never figured out I should have been thanking them for not leaving.

Rennie concluded her flowery speech by swearing again on the life of Betsy Ross, though Hal's single head-nod was far more convincing than her thousand-word oath. But I did not care about Hal. As far as I was concerned, he was going to have to proceed with his irresponsible life under the control of Reynolds Brentwood, and Reynolds Brentwood under the control of me. And though I knew my power would not hold up very long after Rennie's remorse faded, I hoped she would behave herself until time for Raven and Constantia to return. After that, she could go back to Texas where she belonged – I'd joyfully help her pack for the trip – and Hal could return to wherever he came from.

Thus, it was my willingness to forgive my friend, dishonorable though my motive, that got me a measure of peace for a short while after we returned home. I should have known better than to expect good conduct from Rennie for more than a few days. I should have remembered the proven axiom: Honeymoon effects that come with making up after a fight do not last. I wish some wise person like you had been around to remind me of this fact before

I tumbled into the next dark pit. Quite a deep one, too. You know it was if Rennie and her running buddy did the digging.

18

After the pot fiasco and ensuing frenzy of empty apologies and emptier promises, I decided my best bet for making it to the end of the semester with my sanity intact was to ignore Rennie and her boyfriend altogether and concentrate on my own objectives. Student teaching was not easy, but since I have always functioned best amidst difficulty, I found myself doing okay with the current version. With Rennie and Hal feigning good behavior for a time, I admit to experiencing a tad of confusion about how to proceed through untroubled waters. I was not accustomed to easy roads, for as you recall, I had never traveled one. Hardship was all I knew, hardship and the learned ability to derive gratification from it. You could call it my fatal flaw, I suppose. Oh, you say you don't have a fatal flaw? Excuse me while I laugh out loud.

Rennie and Hal. Hal and Rennie. What can I say about those two partners-in-crime who resided so blissfully under my bliss-less roof? In spite of their fevered post-New-York assurances of improving their behavior – assurances made while still under the influence,

I later realized – they did not venture far into the noble land of virtue. Granted, I never had to deal with marijuana again, but that did not stop Rennie from dreaming up other ways to annoy me – borrowing my best clothes without asking, playing sitcoms and true crime shows on TV around-the-clock, never cracking open a textbook. And Hal, as low a profile as he kept personally, continued to follow Rennie down her various primrose paths. For a time, he and she both made a joint effort to avoid me. But since the cottage was small and I was super-sensitive to infractions, there was no way I could disregard the myriad of irritants my houseguests generated – cooking when it was time to be sleeping, sleeping when it was time to be cooking, coming and going at all hours, playing every kind of music known to man on the old boombox Hal had brought with him, his only possession other than a few items of faded clothing. He was finishing up a class in musical genres that semester, which meant I found myself trying to work at the computer to background Musak of every sort – orchestral classics, jazz solos, R&B hip-hop, Gregorian chants. Never again will I be able to bear the melancholy of blues improvisations, Hal's listening fare the week prior to Florida and the shooting.

Still, with the exception of said trivial irritations, life rocked along so smoothly for a couple of weeks that I became suspicious of the fates. But then, as I am certain you have predicted, the dissolution of normality came screaming around the corner to remind me of a cold hard fact: Rennie and Hal had no concept of the importance of keeping one's life in strict order for the sake of one's children. No concept whatsoever.

Here's how the next disaster unfolded: Since Rennie was still in bed on Saturday morning by the time I had to leave for Columbia to chip away at the dreaded practicum, I jotted a quick note and taped it to the fridge. In it I explained I had to work with rare materials at Cooper Library that could not be checked out, which would take all day and part of the evening, and I would spend the night in a motel in Columbia to avoid being on the highway late again. It was not an unusual occurrence. I did have to study sometimes for prolonged periods at Cooper if the research tangle I was trying to sort out got complicated. The first time I stayed overnight, though, I did not bother to leave a message, whereupon

Rennie asked me on my return who I thought I was, an inconsiderate teenager? She said she had worried herself sick I was dead in a ditch somewhere and was about to call the police and report me missing.

From then on, I let her know my plans. The problem on this particular Saturday was that I forgot to inform her I had changed them. I did not realize if sneaky Rennie believed I would not be home for the night, she and Hal would throw the wildest party Sullivan's Island has ever witnessed.

I won't go into the details of my research project (as you recall, it was in fact my professor's project, the one he had laid on me like a first-class jerk), the bulk of which had to be done in Columbia. Let's just say it had to do with oral histories describing the devastating effects of the infamous boll weevil infestation on cotton growing and textile mills in the state of South Carolina at the turn of the twentieth century, and the toll it took on public education.

After I had listened to a dozen tape-recorded accounts of the boll weevil horror, I began longing for my own bed, not some lumpy, weevil-infested mattress in a roadside motel. Unable to take one more heart-wrenching story of what poverty had done to children back in the day, I dried my tears, packed up my research materials, and left Mr. Boll Weevil and his evil minions in the stacks of Cooper Library.

It was the right decision. Surprisingly, the drive back to Sullivan's turned out to be pleasant. Nonstop oldies-but-goodies on radio stations along the Interstate made me forget the pain of the present and find solace in memories of my youth…no matter how revisionist. By the time I rolled across Middle Street on the island, I had shed most of my study tension. No more boll weevils. No more woes. No more worries. I had nothing in my head but the sweet hope of a steaming mug of herbal tea and my own comfortable bed.

All that was before I saw the patrol cars. When I arrived at Station 22 and headed toward the Atlantic Ocean, a parked squadron of blue-lit cruisers greeted me. A terrible crime must have been committed, I thought. Was everything under control now? Were Rennie and Hal okay? I was glad Raven and Constantia were not at home. Otherwise, I would have already been out of the SUV and running toward the cottage since too many official vehicles were blocking me from getting any closer on wheels.

From my distant position, I could not see the actual problem. I pulled off the road and stopped, let down the driver's side window, switched off the Explorers' engine, and waited. Better to assess things before deciding on a course of action. A few curiosity hounds scurried along the roadside toward the police presence and main scene, but they were slowed by a hoard of Philistines hurrying from the opposite direction. I watched this pedestrian traffic jam a few seconds before leaning out my window and asking one of the youthful escapees what was going on.

"Same old thing," the boy said, breathless from having to drag his female companion along by her arm. I assumed she was his girlfriend. She looked young and impaired...by alcohol, most likely. It unsettled me when she slumped to her knees next to my car window, though her protector had no trouble hauling her back to her feet. From all appearances, it was not the first time he had been forced to execute this same move on her behalf.

I accosted him again as he struggled to get his lady turned in the correct direction to flee. "Hey," I said. "What's happening up there, all those blue lights?"

"Police pigs," he muttered half to himself, half to me. "They never want us kids to have any fun." He spoke louder to the girl. "Come on, Tammy. Your mama's gonna kill me if the cops pick us up again." He glanced at me with a see-what-I-have-to-put-up-with look in his eyes, then said with pure disgust for the entire criminal justice system, "They're arresting people left and right back there. I have to get her home. She's underage."

I watched as he towed his drunken little sweetheart away from what looked like hell's own ballroom up ahead. Yes, her mother may very well kill him. And then it came to me in a brain blast that the fun he was referring to had been going on in my own home. A half-dozen police cars had their front ends pointed directly toward the cottage.

I got out of the Explorer and began walking at a brisk clip toward the circus of flashing lights. Somebody, two somebodies, must have thrown a party while I was away, the aftermath of which was playing out badly right in front of my eyes. Welcome home!

As I neared the driveway, an officer in uniform stopped me; "Can't go no closer," he said. "Wait here by my car while I deal with these other two idiots."

He had detained a different boy and girl, college material from the looks of their clothing, and was writing them citations without the slightest concern that the girl was howling like a wildcat.

I asked the officer if whatever had gone wrong was breaking up now. He said as he continued writing, "Won't be much longer. Things like this usually settle down after the student punks take off. Neighbors are still riled, though. Been calling the station about the noise, the fire, whatever. One old geezer swore up and down he heard gunshots. Dispatcher sent me and my partner over to investigate. The party had moved outside by the time we got here. Some dumbass started a bonfire in the backyard…sparks flying in every direction. Had to get a fire truck to come out, lights and sirens. Didn't want the neighbors' houses going up. It's always about the neighbors on these islands. I know. I live on one myself."

As he talked, I squinted toward the epicenter of the maelstrom. Was that Rennie? Rennie and Hal, standing at the top of the street-side steps of the cottage next to the kitchen door? Yes, sir, there they were on the postage-stamp landing talking to yet another gentleman-in-blue. And though I could not hear a word they were saying, it was clear from Rennie's gesticulations, she was making a bad situation worse. The officer who had taken charge of me continued scribbling on his notepad. How was I going to get away from him? And why-oh-why couldn't Rennie take a lesson from Hal, who was standing by motionless without speaking?

Try as I might, I could not extricate myself from my new compadres – teenage boy, teenage girl, and twenty-something rookie cop – until the girl slumped in a dead faint against the officer's chest, knocking his pen and pad out of his hands. While he was sidetracked by the highlight of his night (dealing with an unconscious girl slobbering all over his polished badge), I slipped away from the current absurd scene and hurried toward another, this one playing out on my own stair landing. No need to worry about drawing attention to myself along the roadway. Everyone I passed was embroiled in some drama of their own, making it relatively easy to thread my way around more squad cars, more officers, and many more distressed party guests, plus a twin set of black Labradors from down the street who had escaped their fenced yard and were now dancing around and barking their heads off at the flash-mob now fleeing Peregrine cottage, the quaint little island dwelling that was not really mine, and never would be, and could be taken away as a residence at any moment that Grayson Lockwood Pinckney IV determined I was an unfit occupant. Which had been inching toward the realm of possibility ever since Rennie's return to the East Coast and Hal's arrival from who-knew-where.

Rennie, my quasi-criminal friend, and Hal, her paramour, beheld the savage look in my eyes the second I started my climb up the outdoor stairs. They scrambled to get behind the police officer, assuming correctly he was the lesser of two evils. Hal appeared on the verge of sprinting past me down the steps and disappearing into the night, given half a chance, which the officer and I made sure he did not get. As soon as I got close enough, I seized Hal's muscled arm and dug in my nails. He yelped, but did not defend himself. I tried to get hold of Rennie's arm with my other hand, but she lurched just out of my reach and cowered behind the policeman. Each time I stepped to the right or left, she would duck in the opposite direction. The young cop endured this a second or two before figuring out what was going on. Then he jerked around and grabbed the elbow of his plump female detainee and forced her to stand still. I could think of nothing but the TV crime shows Rennie had grown so fond of watching over the last few weeks. And how, when the background announcers described in monotone the antics of the offenders, Rennie would double over with laughter and call them ignorant nincompoops, and now here she was, the most ignorant nincompoop of all starring in her own episode.

Hal, who was more my prisoner than the police officer's, could find no opportunity to escape. I held him in a vice-grip as I reached out in one more violent attempt to grab hold of Rennie. The officer, who for some reason took an instant dislike to me, got up in my face and shouted, "Calm down and back off, Miss Bossy Britches or you'll be in cuffs next."

I obeyed, halfway. I backed off, but did not calm down. Rennie smirked at me after the officer's outburst, which made me so angry

I wanted to choke her. But I did not go after her physically again. I jabbed at her with words. "Wipe that look off your face, you... nincompoop. This time I'm not going to going to save your butt."

She leaned around the other side of the officer and glared at me like a disheveled little beast. At that angle, the porch light shone full on her face, the sight of which made me cringe. Her makeup had melted into a Halloween painted face of mascara streaks, lipstick smears, and was that soot on her forehead? Strangely, she did not seem to care, or maybe she didn't realize what she looked like. Whatever the case, she had no trouble defending herself verbally against me, her generous hostess. "What are you doing home?" she said. "You're supposed to be in Columbia. Why do you always say one thing and do another?"

I sharpened the glint in my eyes. "Which is so far beside the point that I won't even address it," I said. Then I shifted my attention back to the policeman. "Are you arresting her? And him?" I pointed to Rennie and then to Hal.

"My cuffs'll fit you, too, lady," he snapped. "Pipe down, or you'll be cooling your heels in my squad car." For reasons I never understood, this barely post-adolescent cop had developed in the shortest time possible more disdain for me than Rennie and Hal. Said he with a mean, squint-eyed face that looked comical on someone so young, "I'm taking statements here, and you, woman, are next in line."

"Me? I didn't have anything to do with this. I wasn't here."

"That's what they all say. Now stand aside and let me do my job."

Again, I shouted at Rennie. "I can't believe I get home exhausted to find you and Hal in the middle of another s-storm. You're right. I would'a been better off staying in Columbia. A guy on the road back there says you came close to burning the cottage down... and the neighbors' cottages."

Rennie sniffed and wiped her face with the back of her hand, a move that blackened her nose with mascara. She was beginning to resemble a puppy. "Things got a little out of hand," she said. "I don't know why. Never did before."

She slunk behind the police officer and pressed close enough to his back to annoy him. He raised an eyebrow and stepped away from her. Hal continued studying his own shoes.

Said I to the guilty redhead, "What do you mean never did before? How many times have you done this? Don't answer. I don't want to know. Columbia is dull. All the fun has been going on at my house. Do you realize this is Raven and Constantia's home? I'm sick of you and your playmate putting them in jeopardy."

Hal spoke then, an event of great interest to everyone present since it was the first time he had opened his mouth. The police officer Rennie was still trying to hide behind turned and stared at Hal. So did Rennie. So did I. Though I was thrown off balance when the new speaker wrenched his arm out of my grasp and stepped closer to me face to face. "Get off Rennie's case," he said. "None of this is her fault. Most of the clowns who showed up here tonight were dumb undergraduates. I don't know how they found out about it. I invited a few of my buddies in the art department and it went from there."

Now then, I feel the need to emphasize at this point that Hal was categorically wrong if he thought shifting the blame from Rennie to himself would make me feel better. No, it made me feel worse. Over the weeks I had known Hal, I had grown to wish for the sake of his own irresponsible self that he would give up thrasher kicks, male ponytails, and inner wrist infinity tattoos, and start acting like an adult. Occasionally, I would see a glimmer of hope he may be inclined, although not on this night. This night I found myself growling through clenched teeth at a young dude obviously still suffering from a galloping case of arrested development. "Have you lost your mind, you overgrown, play-like hipster? I could lose my children over this. If some kid gets killed in a car wreck on the way back to Charleston, and alcohol is involved, and they trace it back here, you and Rennie and I will be blamed straight-up. People have gone to prison for less."

Rennie laid one open hand on her own cleavage and the other upon Hal's forearm. "Don't blame Hal. Blame me," she said.

I gagged on her melodrama as she continued down the same syrupy trail Hal had just blazed. "It was my idea, not his. He looks to me for guidance, 'cause I'm older and smarter and all, but I let him down in a big way tonight. I'm sorry, Hal…Arly. I let you both down."

The gallantry of these two actors made the officer cough to cover a chuckle. But I saw no humor in their antics. I was a hair's breadth from violence myself. "Rennie," I said with an uncharacteristic vocal fry. "I had hoped you were over this kind of thing. It's why I let you come here. What did you think? That I was living the bohemian life on an uncivilized island? I'm a mom now, trying to plan and work and do the right things for my children. Raven and Constantia have to have a stable childhood. Isn't it enough I've got Stuart and Giselle stuck in my craw? Why did you do this to me? And after I've been so good to you."

My old friend screwed up her face and started to cry. She pre-empted me on this. I was about to cry myself. It was then the officer announced he'd had enough, and for everybody to cool it, that situations like this look different in daylight, which from the look of the sky would not be long in coming, and it didn't sound to him like any one of us had a grain of sense, and where were these poor children I was talking about?

"Florida," I murmured, "with their father."

"Not here?" he said, "in this nut house?"

"No, Florida," I repeated. "And these two…" I glanced at Rennie and Hal, both of whom appeared to be drowning in remorse. "…are houseguests. I live here, but I wasn't here for whatever went on tonight. I came up on it a few minutes ago from off the island, same as you."

"Step back," the officer said to me.

I obeyed without hesitation. I'd have executed a perfect cartwheel down the stairs if he had asked. The beleaguered young man was done with crazy-speak and ready to get down to business. His detainees, including me, went silent, our best collective decision for the entire episode. After all, the officer was the only one present in possession of a weapon and a citation pad.

He decided to charge me with nothing, though, as I have already mentioned, he liked me least. Compared to Rennie and Hal, however, my part was small potatoes in this freak show, which was the officer's direct quote in describing the global nature of the situation. The real lawbreakers, Rennie and Hal, had committed so many offenses that it took the weary sergeant several minutes to list them all out. He explained with more haughtiness than was necessary that supplying alcohol to minors was their worst violation, far worse than endangering the property of others and disturbing the peace. I got off with a short lecture on the dangers of allowing alcoholic idiots to set up shop in the home of my children, and next time, if there were a next time, I would have the book thrown at me too. I nodded gratitude and should have felt relief, but my nerves would not let me. What Rennie and Hal had done was no good. Did they not understand the custody implications? Nothing made sense to me anymore. And for a short while longer, nothing would.

I thought things could not get worse. And when the officer departed without taking Rennie or Hal or me with him, I hoped things would get better. But then I entered the cottage and discovered how wrong I had been.

The party guests had trashed the house. Sticky drink cups littered every surface, drawing ants and other creepy-crawlers. The smell of throw-up permeated the air. Cigarettes and skinny cigars smoldered in heavy glass ashtrays in every room. Where, I thought, did Rennie and Hall find heavy glass ashtrays? When I asked, Rennie said they were downstairs in the storeroom in a plastic tub full of assorted party props - red swizzle sticks, plastic ice cubes that glowed in the dark, wine glasses shaped like hula girls, paper lanterns, strings of party lights, outdoor torches – all kinds of neat stuff, depending on one's definition of neat, that had been left there by previous occupants.

The living room was a nightmare, the bedrooms worse, the bathrooms indescribable, and my private bath the most foul of all. One discourteous party guest had been sick on the floor and tried to clean up the mess with one of my best spa towels. But to my astonishment, though not to Rennie and Hal's, the vomit incident was not the capper. The capper was when I came upon a loving couple of the opposite sex sleeping soundly in my own bed. I should definitely have stayed in Columbia.

19

I spent hours cleaning up after Rennie and Hal's little get together. According to talk show psychologists, lots of women clean when they get angry. For whatever reason, it takes the edge off their fury and frustration, feelings I was certain Rennie and Hal were not experiencing. Hal fell in with me on my neurotic cleaning spree for the simple reason that he was a natural domestic. Rennie fell in, too, but out of fear. I did not believe for a minute the two offenders were helping me in order to atone for their sins. No way they were sorry. Sorry they had gotten caught, yes, but not for the deeds themselves.

As I worked, I tried to navigate the cottage via tunnel vision to avoid the sight of my annoying helpers. First I went through the living room and sunroom with a giant plastic trash bag and filled it with debris left behind by the barbarians. Next I vacuumed and mopped both rooms, wiped down all the surfaces, bagged pillows and throws in preparation for a trip to the dry cleaner, and then did what I could for the tortured sofa and easy chairs by spraying them down with fabric freshener to lessen the acrid odor of smoke.

Does contrition have a smell too? In the presence of my delinquents-in-residents, I was beginning to think so. Fumes seemed to emanate from their pores, until I realized the weird new smell was not from guilt, but from a conglomeration of chemical vapors churned up by the hazardous products we were using to sanitize the haired-over space.

I was surprised the dangerous gases did not stop the two culprits from putting their shoulders to the wheel. Rennie, clearly feeling sorry for herself, shed tears as she disinfected toilets, cleaned sinks, mopped bathroom floors, and scrubbed showers and tubs. Hal, unlike Rennie, wasted no strength emoting. He fixed his face in a grim mask and concentrated on his favorite space, the kitchen, scouring it from top to bottom, wall to all, baseboard to baseboard, appliance to appliance, to include the oven in which one of the more sophisticated party guests had roasted raw Brussels sprouts drizzled with garlic butter. Now if you have never encountered the smell of roasted Brussels sprouts sauced with garlic butter, you have not lost the ten years off your life that goes with the experience. This malodorous effort at gourmet cooking was epic in failure. Anyone in his right mind would have known that the crowd of Cretans in attendance at Rennie and Hal's impromptu soiree would not be interested in wholesome hors d'ouvres. Judging from the refuse they had left behind, they were, to a person, skipping down the road to early-onset liver and pancreas disease brought on by the consumption of alcohol and trans fat.

Hal's success in vanquishing the oven debacle cost him plenty. He suffered an hour-long coughing spell from breathing too much aerosol oven cleaner, a product that ought to be legally banned. I gave him a couple of sidelong glances during his marathon hacking, snorting, sneezing, choking episode, though I felt little pity. For Rennie, I felt no pity whatsoever despite her copious crocodile tears.

It took hours of labor on the part of all three of us to wash away the filth in the cottage. My initial intent was to eliminate the physical mess with dispatch, but to let the psychological vibes hang in the air indefinitely. You know…elongate my righteous indignation.

But no one could hate Rennie for long. And I did not know Hal well enough to hate him at all. It made little difference to me if he tried to take the blame for the fiasco. I gave him no credit for chivalry. Besides, I knew it was not his fault, not when Rennie was around to lead the charge. So…when I got over hating Rennie, I got over hating Hal. Why squander emotion on the lesser culprit?

It was predictable the way my disdain for both Rennie and Hal lessened in direct proportion to the increasing cleanliness of the cottage. Hope replaced the odor of Brussels sprouts. Optimism dismissed gloom. Maybe, just maybe, I began to think, the whole episode could be overcome. If I handled things with maturity and aplomb, perhaps I could avoid throwing everyone in the house off track relative to schoolwork, including myself. Should I forgive Rennie and Hal to the purpose of assuring a smooth path home for Raven and Constantia? After a few hours, I started to consider the possibility.

By mid-morning, we had done all we could for the interior. Hal administered the finishing touches by making every ashtray and bar toy disappear downstairs and then wiping down the windows in the indoor common areas with Windex, which erased the lingering funk of cigarette smoke. Oh, excuse me, was I supposed to be grateful for this miracle performed by Hal, when there never should have been lit cigarettes in my home at all? Even on non-party occasions, I required Rennie to go out to the deck to puff away on her vaping machine. She had adopted this habit after committing once in my presence the violation of smoking a real ciggie indoors.

Encouraged by the stellar improvement in the living room and sunroom – now cleaner than they had ever been before – I decided I had the strength to tackle one last nuisance, the ever-present layer of sand covering the wooden skidway to the beach. That it was too early in the day for outdoor work did not matter. Hal was choking me with Windex indoors. A quiet task like sweeping wood slats presented no risk of waking the neighbors at an uncivilized hour, especially the hard-of-hearing Mrs. Lupio. Each stroke of the broom provided therapy for my soul. As I thrashed away at the splintery gray boards, I felt less like thrashing Rennie and Hal's backsides.

When done with the skidway, as well as one can be done with any task involving beach sand, I walked around to the front of the cottage and took a humiliating look at six brown lawn bags lined up street-side in their convicting row. They bulged with crude evidence of the night's not-so-joyful-beer-and-liquor bash. The meticulous Hal had placed the bags side by side next to the green trash bin. The bin, a crude monster issued by the town of Sullivan's Island, had never housed more than a half-dozen, neatly tied-up trash bags each week since I had taken up residence at the cottage four-plus years ago. This morning, however, it strained under the weight of such an astonishing number of un-bagged, empty beer bottles that its hinged lid rested cock-eyed atop the mound.

Fortunately, Monday was rubbish day on the island, meaning all physical evidence of the blowout would be gone by the next afternoon. And more fortunately, there had been enough paper lawn bags hiding in the storeroom beneath the cottage to accommodate the shocking amount of yard debris created by Rennie and Hal's festivities. Otherwise, my shame before the neighbors would have been doubled, tripled, quadrupled.

I sighed again at the sight of the bags, then lifted my gaze to a more agreeable view, the sky full of fluffy clouds that had blown in from the ocean after sunrise. Why is it that mornings of exquisite beauty so often follow wretched nights? After appreciating the smell of clean air a few moments, I stepped to the side of the house where I noticed Hal in the distance raking rubble away from the dunes. Shirt off, sweat plentiful, he was clearing the massive area where the merrymakers had lit last night's inferno. My guess was they had thought to enjoy a picturesque campfire tableau by the sea – roasting marshmallows, singing songs, telling ghost stories. But in their drunkenness, they had let the flames get out of control in the wind, threatening not only the Peregrine cottage (my borrowed home), but neighboring cottages as well. Not to mention everyone's deck and lawn furniture, vehicles, catamarans, fountain statues, and landscaping. This time I let out a groan instead of a sigh.

But back to Hal. I had gotten tired of admiring the beauty of the morning (not a habit of mine on a good day, much less a bad), so I focused on what my contrite housemate was doing. My spectator zone beside the cottage gave me a full view of his project, plus a narrow view of street-side area. I could see parts of both front and back lawns due to a miscalculation by the contractors who had overseen original construction of the cottage. The whole structure had been built too far right on the lot, leaving an awkwardly wide empty space on the left. I decided to have a seat on the skidway where I could rest as I observed Hal. So many hours with no sleep were catching up with me. I could feel the approach of an inevitable crash.

We won't talk about Hal being shirtless. That would be vulgar. We'll talk about my excessive interest in the meticulous manner in which he was picking out the biggest pieces of charred driftwood from the bonfire which had been drowned sadistically by the police officers the very first chance they got. Hal had given up raking for the moment. I now enjoyed watching him make several trips, more than three, carrying loads of black stuff to the street. His efforts to be discreet came off as almost comical. It was quite wily the way he took pains to mix in the burnt lengths of wood with the line-up of fat brown lawn bags, pretending all the while it was normal to have such a quantity of blackened you-name-it amongst one's weekly rubbish.

I groaned again, glad for the sake of the neighbors that he was shirtless. Hopefully, this would take their minds off the shocking amount of trash...the women's minds anyway. It wasn't long before Rennie came moping out to the back deck, saw what Hal was doing, and saw me watching him from the skidway. She crept down the steps to the back lot. I suppose she did not want Hal to get ahead of her in garnering favor from the work gang boss (me). It was the only reason I could think of for her to expend so much energy pulling an old blanket disgraced by the vomit of strangers – seating for the bonfire assembly, I surmised – out to the street and covering a few pieces of blackened wood with it. Her purpose for doing this, she announced, was to keep nosy neighbors out of our business. No use giving them any more reasons to judge us. They've got enough already. I agreed with her, the first time I had agreed with Rennie on anything since her arrival.

Hal worked an hour or so longer around front, including hosing off the parking area and making trips in and out of the storage area downstairs to find tools and such. I had no idea where he had been storing work boots and cut-off Wrangler jeans. But wherever it was, they came in handy for his cleanup duty post-fire. For his finale, he trudged back to the dunes near the ocean where he used the same old rusty rake to mix in white ocean-side beach sand with cinders and ashes left behind by the fire. By the time he completed this clever little deception, that of hiding ashes in plain sight, the remains of the fire were hardly discernible. Only a grayish area halfway between the house and dunes provided weak evidence that a bonfire had ever threatened the lot...unnoticeable unless one knew where to look.

For good measure, he gave the whole area a once-over with the rake before stopping to survey his work. In the middle of scanning for needed detailing, he spotted me sitting alone. I did not acknowledge him. I glared at him. He gestured with a hand toward his grand achievement – the complete elimination of every stinky shred of fire rubble – and waited for my approval. I maintained eye contact for two stony seconds, then I stood up and plodded to the back deck steps. On entering the sunroom, I let the door slam behind me. Hal would have to get his appreciation fix from Rennie.

Who, I discovered, was now taking a break in the sunroom, for hiding amidst the quiet of white wicker and chintz cushions came more naturally to a privileged diva like Rennie than following along behind a roaring vacuum cleaner. Poor, poor Rennie...dirty and pale, with witchy hair and broken nails. This was not the look my thoroughly modern pal paid hundreds of dollars to acquire every week at her favorite hair-and-nail salon in downtown Charleston. My suspicion? This was the first time Reynolds Lucinda Brentwood had ever cleaned a house in her life. For certain, I knew it was the first time she had cleaned mine.

I sat down beside her with no smile or greeting. "I'm going to have to speak to Mr. Pinckney about this," I said.

She nodded and wiped her nose with a bare hand, which widened a smear of soot across her cheek. I got up and went to the bathroom for a damp washcloth.

"Here, wipe off your face," I said on return. "You're a mess. We're both a mess." I paused for a mutual silent moment before continuing. "I don't know what a thing like this could mean for me legally. They fingerprint applicants for state teaching credentials."

Rennie looked puzzled. "You're kidding. Why?"

"It's the law. And I've worked too long and hard trying to meet the requirements to have you and Hal ruin everything. It hasn't been easy studying with the two of you around, and even harder letting Stuart keep Raven and Constantia long enough for me to get through this last leg, all so I can be a responsible mother. And now this. I can't bear to think what Stuart and Giselle might try to do with it."

Rennie began crying again. "Cut it out," I said. "You aren't the victim here. I'm sick to death of you and everybody else playing the martyr. It's like an epidemic coming at me from all sides."

20

By late in the day on Sunday, the party calamity appeared to be dying away. Neighbors and police had gone silent to the point of dropping all charges, Rennie and Hal invisible, and I had returned to my studies with humble gratitude that no one seemed to be interested in threatening my children's future. In the early afternoon, after three hours of prep work on student teaching support materials for the week ahead, I rewarded myself with coffee and a bagel to get me through the last of my preparation marathon.

Rennie and Hal were not at home. They had been making themselves scarce since the party. At times I hardly knew they were still living in the cottage. What I had wanted was to throw them out on their ears immediately, but I relented when Rennie pointed out how close we all were to the end of term, and what a shame it would be, particularly for Hal, to have to find a temporary place to crash while he finished his course work. She offered to go back to Texas forthwith, but pleaded with me to let Hal stay and button up his assignments without having to sleep on a park bench somewhere downtown. Then she began bawling again, lamenting that the best thing would be for her to scratch altogether the idea of trying to get a diploma herself and go home empty-handed like everyone in Dallas expected her to do from the start. What did Texas need with another degreed artist anyway? I surmised that Texas needed all the degreed artists it could get since the extent of my knowledge about the Lone Star State had come from Rennie and Hollywood movies.

Okay, I admit it. My real reason for letting them stay was not magnanimity. The truth was I still didn't want to be alone, not even for three weeks. But I would never have let Rennie know this. I told her she and pretty-boy could show how sorry they were for causing me so much trouble by bringing home straight As on their final exams. She agreed tearfully, and we left it at that.

Now you and I must go back to those quiet hours on Sunday afternoon when I was taking a study break from writing lesson plans and creating teaching aids. It was the classic calm before the catastrophic emotional storm that culminated in two shooting deaths. After a double infusion of the darkest roast coffee for which one can over-pay at the local organic food store, I went downstairs in my usual depressive state of mind to throw a few towels into the washer. It was good to contemplate a task that required no thought, and wonderful to have a reliable idea of what its outcome would be...nothing more than a few clean towels.

After the party, I had begun feeling that something more insidious than surface turmoil might be going on in the cottage, but try as I might, I could not identify its source. I coped by reminding myself I was still the same out-of-step creature I had always been. Not once did I give my qualms credence or connect them with Hal. I had done enough reading about psychology to know that he and Rennie misbehaved around me because I allowed them to. And I assumed, incorrectly, that whatever ill will I harbored toward them sprang from my own inadequacies. But about all this I had been wrong...dead wrong...literally.

As I was leaving the laundry room, which had been the old servants' quarters in the ancient cottage, I tripped over the rake Hal had used to clear away the fire debris the morning after the big event. In my herky-jerky efforts to keep from falling, I came close to upsetting a basketful of clean linen, evidence of the free maid service I had provided for the unknown party animals who had found it convenient to take a nap in my bed. Yet somehow, despite my clumsiness, the neat stack of folded sheets and pillowcases remained lodged inside the basket instead of tumbling onto the sandy concrete. Grateful, I took a wide step around the basket and stood motionless for a moment to regain my balance. That was when I noticed the assortment of yard tools and fishing tackle Hal had left scattered about. I decided if I did not want to break my neck on the next trip down for laundry duty, I needed to extend my study break long enough to put a few things back in place.

The effort of gathering up the tackle box and fishing rod at the same time turned out to be an awkward enterprise. And a whole other struggle ensued when I tried to free up a hand to turn the storeroom doorknob only to find it locked. By this time, I had grown irritated at Hal for leaving all this junk around. It was not in his compulsive nature to do that kind of thing...which made it even more irritating.

I dropped the fishing rod and tackle box to the floor and stomped off to fetch the storeroom key from its hiding place. It should have been hanging from one of six rusty nails on an inside support post for the front steps, all hidden from obvious sight. But when I reached for it, it was missing...no longer with its companions in their shiny line-up – spare house key, Explorer key, laundry room key, and extra gate key to the parking area under the house.

I puzzled over its absence. Had Raven and Constantia snagged it? No, not probable. They were too young to be playing alone in the lower spaces. Hal was the most likely suspect. He spent more time downstairs than anyone else.

I decided to move on to my second hiding place for keys. Stepping from under the slant of the stairway, I strode across the parking area to the Explorer, thinking as I went about how complicated doing the laundry had become. Even so, I was enjoying my superiority to Rennie and Hal. Those two would never have thought to hide a second set of keys. Over the course of my lifetime, I had lost more keys than I'd kept up with, which made me careful as I grew older to take precautions.

I plucked the second set of keys from under the front seat of the Explorer and wasted no time congratulating myself on how smart and proactive I had been to hide them there. How ironic to be thinking such self-aggrandizing thoughts, considering what I was about to discover. I hurried back to the cottage and unlocked the storeroom door, taking care afterward to pocket the keyring to ward off a need for more search-and-destroy missions later on (because I was so smart and proactive and all…not). Then I began gathering up the awkward pile of this-and-that I had been trying to collect and stow away for going on twenty minutes.

It was dark inside the storeroom when I opened the door. I noticed with frustration that it took my eyes longer than usual to adjust to the dim, an unpleasant reminder I was no longer in my twenties. Still, why would the room be so shadowy on such a bright, beachy afternoon. I had forgotten both windows had been painted over from the inside, a custom observed decades ago that would have sent any modern decorator into clinical depression. I recalled from other visits to this lonesome chamber that a naked light bulb operated by a chain-pull hung from the ceiling. But as things were going, the pull would most likely be corroded to the point of useless. I never expected it to work on the first try, but to my utter amazement, it did.

The blare of the bulb jarred me as much as the tidiness of the room. It looked nothing like the hopeless hodge-podge of the laundry area. Someone with Hal's type-A personality had arranged the stored items into displays reminiscent of garage sale exhibits. Beach toys, exercise equipment, yard tools, water rafts, and other articles looked as if they were enticing customers at a bargain basement sale. Some items rested on wall shelves. Others hung from giant hooks on pegboards. Bigger objects such as bicycles, lawn mowers, and float toys rested in quiet repose on the gritty floor beneath the shelving.

I'd had no reason to visit this room in weeks, not since Rennie's arrival, nor Hal's. Storerooms were of no concern to me. Nothing occupied my mind but schoolwork and worries about Raven and Constantia, the two reasons I did not care when Hal staked his claim on the downstairs. It happened over time, starting the morning after his first sleep-over. He went outside early, coffee mug still in hand, and took a leisurely stroll around the front and backyards. I watched him from a sunroom window as he scrutinized the sandy areas in the manner of a professional landscaper calculating a quote.

After a lengthy perusal, he set his mug down on the skidway and disappeared into the garage area beneath the cottage. A few minutes later he emerged carrying assorted garden tools and began edging, weed eating, and trimming the overgrown foliage. Unlike Rennie, Hal seemed to have a desire to earn his keep. I supposed it was the reason he established his ongoing relationship with the outdoor regions of his free dwelling place. Within a week, he had managed to get the overgrown hedges under control, weed every green area that needed weeding and some that didn't, and edge the driveway to surgical precision. He also busied himself with hosing off the driveway and concrete slab under the house, both of which could turn into daily tasks for a compulsive type like Hal…and also sweeping the endless layers of sand off the steps and walkways and skidway, mowing the weeds that stood in for grass, and watering every greenish thing in sight. Some parched brown plants I had thought were terminal came back to life under his care in a remarkably short amount of time. Yes, seaside homes do have sandy/windy/work-creating disadvantages that most people do not want to include in their dreamy ideas of how wonderful it would be to own one, yet none of those intimidated Hal. He addressed every job with grand success. And though I noticed his varied achievements, I withheld outward gratitude. Let him work his rear end off, I told myself every time I saw him tramping toward the street with a lawn bag filled with clippings. I do the laundry, don't I?

I did not know he had conquered the storeroom. From the look of things in that echo space, he had been spending more time downstairs than I realized. I hoped the laundry room would be his next project. It gave me a pang to see Raven and Constantia's water toys hanging from large pegs. I would rather have found them drying on the deck from recent use. And I felt worse on lowering my gaze to the shelf crammed full of multi-colored buckets and shovels. The girls' toys were a heart-breaking reproach to my decision regarding extended visitation with Stuart and Giselle. I picked up a bucket and found myself forcing back tears at the sight of Constantia's artwork on the exterior. She had used permanent markers to paint a large red heart with stick figures on either side, one with yellow hair, the other with black.

I set the bucket down and wiped my eyes, unwilling to give in to weakness of any sort that might hinder my progress in bringing my little ones home. Three weeks, I whispered aloud. Less than three weeks. It took effort to project my mind into that sublime future in which I would be finished with student teaching, officially degreed and certified, and reunited with my children. "Stick to the plan," I said to myself. "You can make it."

Tears I could not control burned my cheeks as they dried in salty streaks. I scrubbed at them with a rough hand before reaching for the chain-pull to turn off the ceiling light. Time to hit the books again. Stay focused.

But just before pulling the chain, I allowed myself a last look at the girls' toys. It turned out to be of monumental importance, this insignificant glance, one that changed my life forever. For my gaze did not fall upon Raven and Constantia's red and yellow buckets and shovels, but on an unfamiliar blue tarp that covered a boxy something on the floor. I stared at it, unsure what it was, where it had come from, who had put it there (Hal most probably).

I walked over and leaned down to inspect the unfamiliar item more closely. On lifting the tarp, I saw that the object underneath was a metal footlocker, the kind children sometimes take to summer camp. It looked new, though cheap and flimsy, with little to indicate that anything inside would need to be secured by the padlock looped through its front catch.

I jiggled the lock. Rennie had not brought anything like this from Texas. That I knew for certain. Footlockers were not her style, not expensive enough. Which left Hal as its potential owner. I stared at the shiny new lock, considering whether I had the right to break it.

My brain began rationalizing. I know it isn't mine. But the storeroom is, in a way. Don't I have a responsibility to check out any suspicious container that shows up in my home...for the safety of my children if nothing else? Think of the legal risks Hal and

Rennie have already introduced. I'd be crazy not to monitor every little thing. What if this trunk is full of marijuana...or worse?

I knelt and worked with the lock long enough to know it was not going to open without brute force. That was when I removed a claw hammer from its pegboard hook and gripped its wooden handle with my right hand. After the second unsuccessful blow to the padlock itself, I stared in disbelief when the thin metal plate securing the lock to the trunk gave way. Two screws fell to the floor, and the plate slipped sideways. Strange. The padlock itself remained tightly locked, but the trunk was now unsecured. I laid the hammer on the floor – you are right, it never made its way back to the pegboard – and gave the padlock a sharp tug, at which point the plate's other two screws popped out and the entire apparatus fell into my hand. I turned it back and forth, perplexed by its worthlessness despite being obviously new. Then I laid it on the floor next to the hammer.

Inside the trunk, I found nothing of interest, just textbooks and more textbooks arranged in neat stacks, each one evidence of Hal's studies: Music Appreciation, Art Appreciation, Art History, Technical Aspects of Drawing, Oil Painting, Acrylic Painting, along with a stack of spiral composition binders full of cursive scrawl that looked like class notes. I fingered everything, looked around and between and under the binders, but did not find what I was looking for, that is, drug paraphernalia or actual marijuana. I cannot explain what kind of weird kink in my human psyche made me feel let down. No drugs, no weed, no alcohol, nothing at all incriminating. I knew that for the sake of my children I should have been relieved, yet something about catching the guilty offenders red-handed would have been so satisfying.

I leaned back on my haunches and was about to close the trunk when I realized the upper layers of its contents were resting on a cloth liner midway or so from the bottom. The liner, I discovered, was one of my own black spa towels from the master bath. I had come close to not seeing it due to its dark color, and also because it had been folded into a rectangle that was a perfect fit for the trunk.

All of which sparked my curiosity. What was so important that it had to be hidden under a liner? And who had done the hiding?

I made quick work of lifting out the textbooks and binders and stacking them on the floor. My stomach fluttered as I pulled the towel aside and saw a smaller one of the same color beneath it. Busted, I thought. I've caught them.

The second towel was neither a liner nor divider, but a wrapper of something Rennie and Hal (I assumed) were being oh-so-devious about hiding. I smiled a wry smile, giving in again to the questionable side of my nature that experienced pleasure in finding out the worst about my fellow human beings. Why did it please me to catch my houseguests up to no good? Was I looking for a final excuse to justify kicking them out? Whatever my dark reason, I enjoyed it for the shortest of moments. All my pleasure disappeared in an unwholesome poof when my hand encountered the wrapped lump. I had never touched a firearm in my life, yet I knew what it was the instant my fingers felt its shape within the terrycloth.

I recoiled on unwrapping it, then I dropped it on reflex, towel and all, back into the trunk. Scrambling to my feet, I stood perfectly still without breathing. How did this instrument of death find its way into the storeroom of my sweet little cottage by the sea? What lunatic would bring a dangerous weapon into the home of small children? Not Rennie. Never Rennie. Hal, then. It had to be Hal. No one else had been in the house.

A robot now, I bent over and picked up the gun again. It was small, the grip an excellent fit for my narrow hand, but much heavier than its size would suggest. I turned it over several times, looking for the catch that would open the chamber to make sure it was not loaded. I had seen enough movies to know this was the first step. Finding its cylinders filled with bullets made me recoil a second time. My breath became shallow and ragged as I snapped the gun shut again – still loaded – and placed it on the floor next to the claw hammer, quite the weak sister by comparison as weapons go. I then felt around in the bottom of the trunk for the presence of any other horrifying thing, like more ammunition. My fingers found the outline of a brick-sized box, also surprisingly heavy when I lifted it out. I knew it was packed with bullets. What other horror would have been inside?

I thought about the relative innocence of a few ounces of marijuana and wished I were holding a wooden rasta pipe instead of an ominous box of ammunition. My ugly wave of gladness at catching someone doing wrong had turned into sweaty fear. I had to sit down before I fell down, indeed, before I fainted. The heavy brick of ammo still in my hands, I sank back to the unforgiving concrete and leaned against the open trunk to perspire my way through a bout of nausea. Placing the box beside me, I covered my face with my hands to think. I had to do something...what, what, what?

I looked back into the trunk and saw another pile of notebooks, ones that had been hidden at first by the gun and box of bullets, but were now visible. They were not stacked neatly like the others, their glossy surfaces providing no traction for staying put. So that under them I could see the edges of something I had not noticed before, a brown portfolio, the kind with a flap held shut by a string that wound around a plastic disc attached to the front. With no reason for doing so except to take my mind off the real problem – that is, someone, Hal being the most likely someone, stashing a loaded gun in the home of children without informing their mother – I picked up the portfolio and opened it, never suspecting its contents would alter the course of my life and the lives of Raven and Constantia forever.

21

I closed the trunk lid and sat on it to concentrate on unwinding the portfolio string. The loosened flap of the cover startled me by popping up and revealing my own name scrawled in red marker on its underside. As I stared at the irregular lettering, a nerve-crawler inched up my spine. This must be it, I remember thinking, the doorway to no return. Shall I step through?

Hands trembling, heart pounding, I slid my hand into the portfolio and pulled out the single item it housed, a black spiraled notebook, again labeled with my name, again in red marker. Chilled, yet perspiring in a drop-sweat, I began my terrifying review. It took a few seconds to work out that what I held in my hands was a journal, a detailed chronology kept by Hal. According to his dated entries, he had begun recording it before he ever moved into the cottage, before meeting Rennie, or me. But why? Why would he do that? How would he know who she was, or who I was?

The first page was a copy of a letter written by Hal to Stuart. Hal knew Stuart? How could Hal know Stuart? The letter outlined an agreement between them:

> Dear Dr. Prince,
>
> I have decided the best way to document your ex-wife's activities is in journal form. That way I can send you dated copies periodically. The money you are paying me is a huge help. Before I met you, I had no idea how I was going to fund the rest of my education. Thank you again for hiring me.

Hiring him? What was Hal talking about?

> You're paying me well, Dr. Prince, and I want you to know I intend to earn every dollar. I've slept over in the cottage four nights so far and haven't seen your ex-wife do anything a judge would say was out of the way. To tell you the truth, all she does is study. But I'll keep watching until I find something incriminating. And if I don't, I'll make something up. Rest assured, I'll keep you informed.

I gasped. Something incriminating? Hal watching me? For Stuart?

> Sunday, my fifth day in the cottage: I'm doing great with Rennie. She likes me, and if I keep being nice to her, I think she'll ask me to move in free and clear. It might take a while, but I think I can make it happen. And if I do manage to stay in the cottage for the balance of the semester, I know I'll be able to find something you can use. I understand why you want to have your children in your own home permanently, and I want you to know I'm doing everything I can to help you accomplish that.

Crazed with anger, I flipped through page after page of the binder, reading some parts, skimming others, grinding my teeth, breathing like an animal caught in a trap. Every detail was there: the marijuana episode, copies of the police report from the party at the cottage with a full description of the fire incident, a fax from Stuart dated early in the semester stating how relieved he was that someone named Hal Lanson – Who was Hal Lanson? Was Morris not his real last name? – had moved into the cottage, and it did not matter whether he was sleeping with Rennie or me. If it came down to it, he (Hal Lanson?) would swear he was sleeping with both of us, a living arrangement no family court judge would tolerate for a custodial parent. And another letter dated after the NYC trip stating the same thing and rambling on in a long, inaccurate narrative about the marijuana escapade. According to this account, taking the stuff to New York had been my idea, and Hal and Rennie had gone along with it to strengthen Stuart's lawsuit for custody. According to Hal, the marijuana affair in New York, in conjunction with my penchant for wild parties and mànage á troi trysts, should be enough to build an airtight case. Stuart agreed in typewritten follow-up notes with everything Hal wrote, emphasizing that he (Hal Morris? Hal Lanson?) must remain a live-in at the cottage as long as possible to establish credibility as an eyewitness.

I stood up, an unconscious act triggered by shock. Nothing that had ever happened to me compared to this…this…all-out effort to take my children. Not being abandoned by my mother and father, or accused of killing Miss Peregrine, or even living with suspicions about Stuart's involvement in her murder…nothing. As I stood there and absorbed into my being Stuart's fundamental betrayal (Stuart, the man who had once claimed to love me), plus the unadulterated treachery of Giselle and Hal, my shoulders began shaking with sobs. I cried at first from hurt, but in seconds, my hurt morphed into fury the likes of which I had never experienced before, and the power of which produced a stunning clarity of thought. I realized for the first time that Stuart and Giselle wanted sole custody of Raven and Constantia so badly they were willing to go to any lengths to get it. And I had been naïve enough to help them.

Without stopping to factor wisdom into my next series of actions, I moved forward on adrenaline. As you know, I have never been a wise woman, only a driven one, a fact that did not bode well for my rivals in Florida. I was conscious of what was going on now, what had been going on all along. Those few cold moments of lucid thinking tightened my whole being around a single compulsion, the need to rescue my children. I felt abnormally strong. Would that I'd had a plan of some sort, or at the least a cool-headed advisor like you to set me on the right course. Tycie had tried to advise me; Rennie would not have known how; and sadly, I had no one else to turn to, not even Mr. Pinckney, who had stopped practicing law altogether after taking on the responsibility of managing Miss Peregrine's estate.

A strange calm settled over me as I slid the dreadful journal back into the portfolio, secured the string, and laid the entire packet on the trunk lid beside me. I stared into space a full minute, curling and uncurling my fingers, clenching my jaw. My gaze gradually found its way back to the gun on the floor. It still lay in full menace next to the hammer and box of bullets. I was now able to see the sleek Smith & Wesson for precisely what it was, not a mere symbol of violence, but violence itself. I bent down and reached for it, withdrew, reached again, withdrew again. Unable to tolerate the feel of cold steel in my bare hand, I picked up the portfolio and placed it beside the box of ammo on the floor, opened the trunk lid again, and took out the smaller towel. It took some manipulating, but I kept at it until I got the two untouchables, gun and ammunition box, wrapped tightly enough in the hand towel to manage them as one item to transport. This left my other hand free for the portfolio, which I retrieved from the floor and held tightly against my body.

Oh, what horrible baggage I carried out of the storeroom that day. Nothing normal like clean towels, only misery and sorrow and heartache. Yet I moved forward with uncommon confidence, a mechanical woman with a bizarre mission. Was this the real me or some hopped-up version of the study-drudge I had always been, a drudge so distracted she would forget to turn off the storeroom ceiling light and close the door. No more time for humdrum tasks. The mechanical-woman/study-drudge had a speeding freight train to stop...Stuart and Giselle's mission to steal her children.

⌘ ⌘ ⌘

Guns, ammunition, and portfolio in hand, I climbed the stairs to the back door of the cottage, entered its extremely clean kitchen, and without slowing down, walked straight to the wall phone by the bar. But as I keyed in Stuart and Giselle's number, a debilitating weariness overtook me. No more adrenaline rush. No more false strength fueled by anger. I slumped onto the stool nearest the phone and closed my eyes, waiting for someone to answer. Giselle picked up after three rings. I knew she would. Stuart had told me her chief aim in life was to keep him away from the phone. Occasionally she would let the maid answer, who'd repeat my name in an accent whenever I divulged it, which was Giselle's signal to snatch the receiver away and begin punishing me over the line with a walloping portion of fake-sugar.

But on the day of the gun, I cut Giselle's performance short. "Put Stuart on," I said in a serrated rasp.

She sugared on, undeterred by the butcher knife in my voice. "Listen, Arlena. I know you don't mean to, but you always call at inconvenient times. Stewy can't talk now. He's outside playing with the children on the pool deck. So cute...building a fort out of lounge chairs and beach towels. He'll call you back tonight after the girls are in bed."

My tone went from harsh to hostile. "No, I have to talk to him now. It's an emergency. I'm on my way there."

The knife-edge succeeded across three states and six hundred miles in nicking Giselle and drawing blood. She dropped off the line. Silence, the ticking of four seconds, then Stuart's voice blaring nasty and loud into my ear. "What's the matter with you, Arlena? You've upset Giselle, made her cry."

"Where are Raven and Constantia?" I said.

"At their Grandma Helen's having a Raggedy Ann tea party and playing in her condo pool. What's going on? You sound...off."

"I thought they were building a fort on Giselle's pool deck. I don't know how the two of you keep up with so many photo ops. And for the last time, the woman you call Grandma Helen, on whom I've never laid eyes, is not their grandmother. She's Giselle's mother and no kin."

"Arlena, I don't want to hurt your feelings by saying Helen is better than the nothing in the way of a grandma you and your own non-family have to offer. Call back tonight. You don't want to talk to the girls when you're like this. You sound awful, really."

"Pack their things, Stuart. I'm driving down to get them."

Stuart's breathing approached wind tunnel velocity. He was so angry he could not speak. I responded to his obscene-phone-caller breathing into the phone by yelling at him. "Did you hear me? You and that child thief you live with can expect me by eleven. Your plan to take Raven and Constantia is in the toilet."

"You listen to me, and listen good," Stuart said when he found his voice. His use of the word, good, pricked my ears, a peculiar error for a former English professor. But I did not correct his grammar. I listened...good. "Arlena? Are you still there? You'd better be. I was going to call you tonight after Rennie had time to get back to the cottage. I didn't want you to be alone when I broke the news. No easy way to say it. Giselle and I are taking the girls to Europe tomorrow. We're already packed and ready. You told me you wouldn't be through with student teaching for three more weeks, and Rennie and that boyfriend of hers would be taking exams the week after. None of that matters now, though. By this time tomorrow, Raven and Constantia will be at Disney in Paris. I don't know what blistered your brain today, but don't bring it down here."

"You can't take the girls out of the country without my permission. I'm their mother. That's kidnapping. And they don't have passports."

"Oh yeah? Sort of like you couldn't let them be born and live out the first two years of their lives without telling me, their father, they even existed? You may as well know, we're suing you for custody, sole custody. Giselle and I think it would be best for the girls to live with us full time. I – we – want what you've already had, years of unbroken time. And what would it matter to you anyway? You just want to hole up in some library and do whatever it is you do in those dust caves."

There he was again, the peculiar English professor, this time admitting he hated libraries. But wait, there was more to his current rant. Said he to the shell-shocked me, "Why don't you stop posing, pretending you like having kids around. That's the real reason you let us have them."

"You can't take my children. I won't let you."

"They're my children, too, and they have passports now. Contrary to whatever fiction you've convinced yourself of, I love them as much as you do. And it's my turn to have them."

"Stuart, listen to me, and listen good. I'll be in Winter Park in six hours. And when I get there, you'd better have Raven and Constantia ready for the drive back."

22

Momentum kicked in as I ran toward the Explorer in the driveway, slid into the driver's seat, and slung my purse to the floorboard on the driver's side. The rest of my cargo of horror...gun, ammunition, and portfolio...I placed with care on the seat beside me. Comfortable passenger seat of the sturdiest vehicle on the market, able to transport anything and anyone. That was how the salesman had described the versatile SUV to me on the day I purchased it. Transport anything and everyone, indeed. I blinked at how shocked he would be to find out the "anything" he spoke of would include a loaded gun, bullets, and a portfolio of plans to steal two children, not to mention transporting their crazed mother to Florida where she intended to stop at nothing to get them back, all on a sunny afternoon in the sleepy south.

I began my drive a few minutes past four. For the first hundred miles, I let the gun stay beside me on the car seat, the loaded gun. I had not had time for safety precautions, and after a while the truckers en route began making me nervous. I became afraid one of them might peer down into the passenger window of the SUV, spot the loose handgun, and go mad with the hope and joy that for once something exciting may happen on a long haul. A bored trucker could radio his contacts, and they could radio theirs, and CB chatter along I-95 would be about little else for a while. I wondered if truckers ever discussed via CB radio the women they saw driving alone on Interstates, alerting each other of their presence, watching to ensure their safety. I have never been afraid of truckers. I've always respected them, counted on their presence for security. But I did not want them knowing a lone woman driving on the Interstate had a gun at the ready. If that happened, blue lights and a search of my vehicle by state troopers would be immediate.

Two hours into my journey, I reached over and moved the Smith & Wesson - S&M .38 to be exact - to the floorboard on the passenger side. It was not easy while driving to maneuver my purse on top of it, but I managed somehow on peril of a smash-up. Two drivers blew their horns at me for weaving, inspiring a self-lecture. You have to stop calling attention to yourself. Stay alert. Stuart and Giselle will win if you get caught speeding toward Florida on a suspicious mission with a loaded weapon in your car.

By force of will I settled my nerves and refocused on my priority, getting Raven and Constantia back home. In an effort to hang onto my determination during the long numbing hours, I re-played in my mind the worst conversations I'd had with Stuart over the last two years. Disgust washed over me as I listened to him press for opportunities to show me how sincere he was, that all he wanted was for the two of us to work together to create a family because he loved me more than anything in the world and had not realized it until after our divorce, and how he realized for certain when he found out about the twins that we needed to reconcile and live our lives together. To keep my anger burning bright, I allowed Stuart's false sentiments bang around inside my head like loose bullets.

"I love you, Arlena. I've always loved you." Cruel words, cruel deceptions. My mind never seriously bought into their deceit, yet my vanity basked in the attention. How stupid that was. Even then, I knew his motive. He wanted more access to Raven and Constantia, and if it meant flattering me, his ex-wife, to get his way, flattering his ex-wife is what he would do in addition to anything else he could think of to insinuate himself back into her life and the lives of the children. And he did not stop after marrying Giselle. Every few weeks I had to suffer him asking if I'd changed my mind about our future, suggesting all I had to do was to say the word, and he would leave Giselle in a heartbeat. But his declarations were lies. He wanted Raven and Constantia, not me. And he wanted them at any cost, a reality I had not fully grasped until I was forced to confront its certainty in the storeroom of the cottage.

I was doing such a good job at keeping my mind jacked up with inflammatory memories of Stuart as I drove along that I was able to get by with only two pit stops. The first was to fill up with gas at a Georgia convenience store, use its restroom, and purchase a few bottles of water. The second was at a truck stop south of Jacksonville. There I took another bio break and bought a chocolate bar. I had promised myself a sugar fix if by some miracle I made it without incident across the Main Street Bridge in Jacksonville.

When I reached the far side of the bridge and rolled onto the South I-95 exit ramp, I was so relieved to be on the last leg of my journey, I shed tears. But I also felt apprehensive because as anyone who drives long distances knows, the last few miles are the most dangerous. I hugged the straight-away of I-95 another hour before the first Disney billboard caught my eye. Thank you, thank you, I breathed when Orlando and environs came into my sights. It was then I began watching for exit signs to the small town of Maitland. The last thing I needed was to miss that exit and have to lose time doubling back. The road to Maitland was also the quickest route to Winter Park, the place I was trying to reach. Beautiful Winter Park, rich with lakes and live oaks, inhabited by the trendiest population in Central Florida...except for the two vile fiends holding my children hostage.

Over most of the miles, I had kept Hal's gun out of sight and Hal himself out of my thoughts. What I had read in his journal was too painful to contemplate. Or was it Stuart's gun? Not that I cared who owned it officially. Rescuing Raven and Constantia was my purpose, even if it meant driving long hours in the company of a firearm of questionable ownership. But why (I'm sure you are asking yourself this same question by now) did I bring the gun along at all? Was my purpose more sinister than just getting it out of the dwelling place of my children? Was my intention to turn it over to Stuart? Or perhaps... Oh, for heaven's sake, what is the point of play-acting at this late date? The reason I brought the gun was to use it...not shoot it, mind you. I never meant to do that. But to brandish it in Stuart and Giselle's faces if they made the mistake of trying to thwart me. A loaded gun in the hands of a mother being denied her children would give anyone pause. My hope was that just showing them I had a handgun would speed up the process of getting Raven and Constantia safely into the Explorer and back to Charleston. My thought was to arrive at Stuart and Giselle's front door, behave in an unstable manner – in hindsight, no act – flash the gun once or twice, demand to have my children back, receive them, and depart. End of story.

As I rehearsed the closing scene of my plan mentally, I always ended its final moments with my tossing the gun from the window of the Explorer at Stuart's feet right where he stood in the driveway, and then peeling out with a screech of tires. But as anyone could have predicted, the actual finale played out quite differently.

23

I reduced the speed of the Explorer on entering Winter Park proper, heeding the warning of a newspaper article I had read recently about police officers in small towns making it their business to know who should and should not be out and about in the wee hours of morning and going to great lengths to check out unfamiliar vehicles. I did my best to keep a low profile on the tree-lined streets and avenues of the picturesque town, though I could not help having to navigate a few of them more than once to get my bearings. Five large lakes within the city limits forced roadways to hug various shorelines in unexpected curves instead of following straight lines and ninety-degree angles of the traditional block system. After numerous twists and turns, I began to wonder if I were in the right municipality, much less right neighborhood.

I was about to give up on finding Palmer Avenue, had already driven by Rollins College twice and the purple-and-pink Seven Eleven three times, when my headlights picked up a corner street sign in the misty darkness. Palmer Ave., it read in bright white lettering against a green background. I swerved wide to the right and thanked the sign itself for its helpfulness. A fresh feeling of exhilaration washed over me when I realized how close I was to my children, though I knew that at night in worsening weather even familiar roads can be tricky. As I turned onto the tree-graced, sidewalk-lined avenue, a wash of gray mist descended like magic from the sky. My exhilaration evaporated as the beginning hints of a headache came skulking to the surface of my brain.

I slowed the Explorer to a crawl and searched for some familiar landmark, hoping against hope to spot the right driveway in front of the right house on the right lake. And then, in the foggy glow of the SUV's headlights, I saw it...Giselle's parents' huge Mediterranean stucco with its wavy, red-tiled roof. Stuart had legitimate bragging rights when it came to the Bordeaus' family home in Florida. "It has more grand oaks than any other property fronting Lake Osceola," he enjoyed proclaiming as if the mighty trees belonged to him and not to his affluent in-laws. He was correct about the property being impressive, especially if you measured it by the age and elegance of its ancient trees.

My new headache bore down with vicious throbbing as I angled the Explorer into the circular driveway. Decorative ground lights on either side of the herringbone brick driveway guided me as I wound my way around to the entrance of the house, where the ostentatious front door, flanked by tall Mexican palms, caused my thoughts to lurch forward. What am I supposed to do now? What if they try to stop me? Why have I forgotten my rehearsed plan?

I glanced in the direction of the handgun on the floor, and though it was too dark inside the vehicle to see it, the knowledge of its presence increased the pounding of my heart. That was the moment I began suffering from a punishing attack of second-guessing. I wished I had checked into a hotel first, gotten some rest, waited until morning. Was I still making bad decisions like I always had? Which was more foolish, letting Stuart and Giselle talk me into an extended visit with Raven and Constantia to start with, or showing up at their front door in the middle of the night with a loaded gun?

What's that you're saying? Why don't I stop adding melodrama to my account? All right, all right. Give me a moment to take a cleansing breath and peel back the layers of self-deception. The fact of the matter was/is this: I knew very well, even in that shaky moment outside the Bordeau front door, precisely what you know now. That I had agreed to Raven and Constantia's extended visit with Stuart and Giselle for my own sake, not anyone else's. I had gotten it into my head there was nothing more important than finishing my degree in record time and getting the girls back home and enrolled in a sweet little school where I could get a teaching job and be near them every day. And I had rationalized away the imprudence of my decision by engaging in untrue, repetitive, time-is-of-the-essence self-talk. I say untrue because time was not of the essence. I could have accomplished everything on my list of goals without giving my children up a single day. True, getting it all done may have taken a little longer under that circumstance, but I could have managed it in the same old regular ways other busy moms manage the impossible.

What an ugly revelation to have to face about oneself, and worse in unfamiliar geographical territory in misty darkness, alone and defeated, in the swank driveway of one's antagonistic ex-husband and his new wife. I felt the malignant ache of regret in my bones. Anyone would have known (as did Tycie, as did I if I had been honest with myself, and now, as do you) that any form of long-term visitation granted to Stuart and Giselle would be a recipe for disaster. Nevertheless, I had ignored common sense and granted it anyway, a reckless decision that had gotten me, and most probably my children, into the worst predicament possible. As I sat shivering in the Explorer in Stuart and Giselle's driveway, I agonized over how to unravel the awful results of my bad judgment.

After minutes of fretting, I killed the engine and headlights and began preparing to do something, anything that would move me closer to Raven and Constantia. The problem was, whether or not you believe me, I did not know where to begin. All I could do was sit there – shallow of breath, clammy of hands and face, sick to my stomach from the worsening headache – and chew my lip. Be strong, I coached myself. One show of weakness, and Stuart will grab the advantage.

I was still trying to force myself out of the SUV when lights blinked on inside the house. Windows on either side of the front door now shone with yellow light. I held my breath as the door swung open revealing Stuart's silhouette on the threshold. He took a half-step forward and waited. I could tell from his stance on the narrow porch that he was studying the situation: misty darkness, impending rain, my vehicle, the distinct possibility I could propose a threat.

I glared at him, forgetting my tendency to make untoward decisions. As always, anger trumped common sense. I reminded myself in vengeful, whispered phrases of the wicked nature of Stuart's motives. Trying to take my children away, making me out an unfit mother, lying about everything.

I leaned over the passenger seat and felt around on the floor for the gun. It's a wonder I did not shoot myself on grabbing it so clumsily and shoving it into the pocket of my sweat jacket. Stuart remained in the doorway, flashlight in hand, still peering in the direction of the Explorer, still considering how to get rid of me with the least effort. He judged correctly not to venture out too far. Considering the complication of the mist, his best defensive position was right where he stood.

Well, I thought, he might have the best defense, but I have the best offense. I shoved the gun deeper into my jacket pocket, inhaled for courage, and opened the door of the Explorer. My left leg buckled as I put my weight down on the driveway's tasteful paving bricks, but I did not let this small fail stop me. Two steps to the left, and I had a clear view of Stuart over the Explorer hood. He had not moved a muscle since appearing in the doorway. After a moment of us staring at each other from a distance, he called out my name. Was that fear in his voice? Cowardice? Weakness?

"I see you, Arly," he said. "Are you alone? I don't know what you expect to accomplish pulling a stunt like this. You must be exhausted, driving all that way."

I remained silent. The sound of Stuart's voice with its false concern and casual tone fueled my anger. I eased around the hood of the SUV, the gun so heavy in my pocket it made my jacket hang lopsided to the right. Stuart shone a flashlight beam in my face, blinding me.

"Stop that," I barked. "You know it's me and you know why I'm here."

He switched off the flashlight and leaned back far enough to place it on a table just inside the foyer, then he stepped further out on the porch, leaving the door ajar behind him. It repulsed me to watch him assume the same arrogant, wide-legged stance I had seen so many times before...shoulders back, fists on hips, chin high. "I told you on the phone. The girls aren't home," he said. "They're at Helen's condo, Giselle's mom. I emailed you after we talked, left voicemails, called Rennie. She was shocked to find out you were driving down here. Don't you ever check your messages?"

"I meant it when I said I was coming to pick up Raven and Constantia. No negotiating."

He went quiet. I could not believe his arrogance. He took out a cigarette and lit it, the lighter flaming orange in the half-light. It was a bad sign, his smoking. I had not seen him do that since the first year we dated. I wished I had a cigarette, too, and a valium and a whiskey...four or five ounces at the least.

I sniffed and barked at him again. "Give me Helen's address, Stu-art." I seared both syllables of his name.

Stu-art took a long drag on his effeminate filter tip. Its coal glowed evil red in the gray mist. Then, striking yet another Lands' End pose, he exhaled an impressive plume of blue-gray smoke, the luxury of which I coveted. He coughed up more smoke before speaking again. "I'm going to say this for the last time, Arlena. Raven and Constantia can't go with you tonight. Giselle and I are taking them to Europe tomorrow...Disney in Paris as you already know. Why not do the smart thing for once, check into a hotel, get some rest. You've got another long drive ahead of you tomorrow."

"I'm not leaving without my children. What you're talking about is kidnapping."

"I'm their father. No one is going to accuse me of kidnapping. I've spoken to you about this on the phone. I've emailed you. I've voice-mailed you. It's documented I let you know our plans."

"Tell me where they are. You're going to be sorry."

"Stop threatening me, you little fake. We're flying out early. And frankly, we don't think it's a good idea for Raven and Connie to see you so close to departure time. No use getting them upset. To tell you the truth, coming here like this...with such a rotten attitude?" He paused meaningfully. "Senseless."

"Don't call her Connie. I'm warning you."

He took another deliberate drag on his cigarette to control the pace of the confrontation. Hindsight would have told him he was wasting his time, but for Stuart, hindsight was not to be.

Exhaustion had rendered me, his adversary, a loose cannon. No one could have predicted what I would do next, except for you, of course. You could have laid out my every move in detail. Oh, how I wish you had been there to stop me.

The next events clocked forward in presto time: Stuart dropped his cigarette to the welcome mat and ground it out with his shoe. If Giselle had lived until morning and observed the smelly butt, she would have had plenty to say about Stuart fouling the pristine decorator mat she and her mother had purchased just the day before at the most expensive home décor shop in Winter Park. If she had lived, that is, which she did not.

After putting the cigarette out, Stuart walked toward me down the porch steps to signal his control of the situation. Then he stopped quite near me and planted his feet wide apart again, this time making a show of staring me down. No matter how hard I tried to hide it, he had succeeded in intimidating me, convincing me in the heat of the moment that I had no choice but to reach inside my jacket pocket and produce the gun. It was a smooth move at first, single-handed. Which did not last long. Almost immediately I had to call the other hand into service to keep the narrow barrel from wavering.

Stuart lost his composure when he saw what he was up against. Shrinking into an ugly crouch, he began sputtering out exclamations. "What? What the hell?"

"Yes," I said. "What the hell?"

24

My wobbly grip on the gun now made it Stuart's turn to feel intimidated. "Go back in the house," I said to him. "You've got five minutes to wake the girls and get them into my vehicle."

"But they aren't here. Seriously…they aren't."

"Liar."

"Lower that cannon, Arlena. You're being weird."

I gave up trying to make him bring the girls to me without force. "Go back in the house…slowly," I said.

He hesitated. I growled. "Move, Stuart."

This time he jumped to obey. I followed him to the door. As we walked, I noticed the night breeze that had been so pleasant earlier was now strengthening. In fact, it was a breeze no longer, but a hostile wind.

Stuart glanced back at me. I gestured at him significantly with the gun. He raised both hands to shoulder level and stepped through the doorway where he turned to face me again and wait for his next order. Amazing, the power a firearm wields. I gestured for him to move back, then I entered the foyer myself, making sure in the process to maintain a safe distance from my foe.

"Close the door," I said. "A storm is coming."

He obeyed with one hand, then lifted it again alongside the other. He spoke, his voice tight with fear. "You've got to know I wasn't lying. They aren't here…really…but if you'll get hold of yourself and give me a chance, I'll call Giselle's mother and tell her we're coming over to pick them up, you and me…together."

A flashback flickered in my brain of the night Louisa Hill had held a gun on Stuart and me at Peregrine House. I recognized for the first time how desperate she must have felt. How cornered. Poor, poor Louisa. Alone and bereft of hope. And now…poor, poor Arlena.

Stuart flinched when I thrust the gun forward again, my behavior not far off Louisa's on her night of despair. "Step back," I said. "I don't trust you. The girls are somewhere in this house…upstairs, probably. Walk toward the back. I see a light on."

Tremors in my arms caused the Smith & Wesson to jerk about. It felt alive and dangerous in my hands. I was having trouble keeping the barrel trained. Why are guns so heavy, I thought? And difficult to control? Moment by moment, my fingers were going numb, though I could not allow Stuart to know. I had come too far to let him overpower me now. The expression on his face told me that he knew I was no longer rational. Fact or fiction, I believed in my heart I was down to my last card, any sane alternative be damned. I had convinced myself Raven and Constantia were in imminent danger, and I was their only hope for escape.

Again the gun wobbled in my hands. I was suffering physically from a cruel combination of exhaustion, over-stimulation, and severe head pain, all draining my strength at the same time. Sweat trickled down my temples, though I shivered as if the air were freezing. My teeth chattered out of control.

It's this house, I thought, this horrible house. On entering the sumptuous living area – vaulted ceiling, grand space, opulent furnishings – I understood why Stuart had been so willing to put up with Giselle. I looked around the room in jerks and stops, my gaze halting on the staircase. Bedrooms, yes, bedrooms are always on the upper floors of McMansions like this. And a bedroom is where

Raven and Constantia would be sleeping at this hour. But how was I going to make it up those wide stair-steps with Stuart at the ready to charge at me?

I was having trouble thinking clearly and more trouble with balance and vision, even hearing. Were there servants in the house? And what about Giselle? Where was she…upstairs guarding the girls? My mind churned. How could I get Raven and Constantia out of bed and into the car without losing control of the gun? Stuart would get the better of me. He'd do anything.

I hesitated; Stuart took a step forward; I took a bigger step back, frightened by the look on his face. It was obvious he was more alert than I, more poised, ready to strike. How had he gotten a handle on things so quickly? I was the one with the gun. Yet I could tell from his face he was counting on me to make some self-defeating error. It was what he was waiting for. And I still did not know if Raven and Constantia were in the house. So many lies had been vomited up. Giselle's lies…Stuart's…Hal's. Lies I had told myself.

My stomach ached. My head ached worse. What was I going to do? How was I going to force Stuart to help me? I found myself having to place my feet farther apart as I tried to think things through. It was becoming difficult to remain upright. I took my left hand off the grip of the gun and brushed my hair out of my face. Stuart took another step closer. He began speaking to me in a patronizing tone as if talking someone down from suicide. His words puzzled me. He was the one on the deadly ledge. Did he not realize that?

"You don't have to do it this way," he said. "Was that a smile on his face? Did he think we were going to have a quiet little chat? He edged nearer. "We can talk it out, honey. We can."

Honey? Talk it out? Tears stung my eyes. "Get back," I said. "Back."

He did not move an inch either way. I was astonished that his arrogance was overblown enough to defy a gun. I was not the only maker of rotten decisions. What a destructive pair we were. A relationship forged in hell. And, unbelievably, nothing of it had changed.

The space in which we were conducting our current, wrong-headed altercation spanned the left wing of the house. A stone fireplace dominated the wall at Stuart's back. It stood at a right angle to a bank of glass doors separating the living area from the terrace and garden. How odd that the large living room was more dimly lit than the outside terrace. A single lamp on a long table behind a sectional sofa provided the only weak beam in the enclosed space, barely bright enough for reading.

But nothing skimpy diminished the outdoor lighting on the other side of the long glass windows and double glass doors. The entire space, all hard-scape and artful flora, shone in the grand glow of open-air floodlights. It was like an expensive, backlit movie set. Hidden ground lights along narrow walkways sent up brilliant bars of color that emerged from groupings of shrubs and palms. Fronds of every length and width shivered in the wind. And, as a gorgeous focal point to draw the eye, two rock-walled pools shimmered with light, the larger pool clearly meant for swimming and the smaller one a matching hot tub. Both had been built to effect a natural look. Not faux in any way, but with underwater lighting that changed colors on a slow timer – green, blue, violet...violet, blue, green. My brief gaze upon this stunning paradise allowed me a view of the thunderstorm's first bright raindrops as they rocketed through the mist, struck the pool surfaces and palm fronds, thumped noisily against glass doors to the sitting room.

It was not until the rain increased in intensity that I glimpsed a green cabana positioned discreetly by the pools. It sheltered a bar and cozy conversation pit littered sadly with an assortment of water toys, the sight of which wrenched my heart. Playthings were out of place in this intricate backdrop that had been designed quite obviously for a well-off homeowner to entertain adult guests – other rich friends, perhaps, or richer enemies, never innocent children.

I shuddered at the charade of a life Stuart and Giselle had fabricated in this showplace. It was a full-out stage play to which Giselle had planned to add, for humanizing effects, two child characters called Raven and Constantia. Lights, camera, action! But wait, from the look of the scattered toys and towels, the overture had already been played and the first act almost over. I did not realize until I saw the elaborate set how late I was to the performance. It is no wonder my children's toys unnerved me. They were

straight forward, her head coming down hard on the edge of her priceless Oriental rug. There'll be blood on the fringe, I thought, and on the Mediterranean tile mosaic. The stain will be permanent in the grout unless an expert comes in and chips out all the squares and re-sets them.

Stuart dropped to Giselle's side. I let go of the gun, the gun that had shot Giselle of its own accord. When it hit the floor, I kicked it away. My hands and heart felt relief at being free of its weight. I flexed my fingers as I watched Stuart work feverishly with Giselle. For a moment, I hoped, pretended, she'd come around, the way a mother would pretend her child who has just been struck dead by a tractor-trailer might wake up. "It's all right, baby," the mother would whimper. "Mama is here. Everything is going to be all right."

But the mother and I were both wrong. Nothing was ever going to be all right again, not on the bloody roadside nor inside the bloody house on Palmer Avenue.

Stuart continued his frantic attempts to revive Giselle. He turned her over, felt for a pulse, listened for breath and heart sounds. He patted her cheek and called to her, "Giselle, Giselle. Wake up, Giselle."

But she did not wake up. She lay still and limp in his arms. I waited, detached, thinking her eyes would blink open momentarily. But they never did. After a time, Stuart gave up trying to bring her around. Then slowly, oddly, he turned his gaze toward me. "What have you done? he whispered. "What have we done. We can't fix this."

Grimacing and dissolving into tears, he slumped over Giselle again and cradled her body. I watched as he hugged and rocked her in a manner in which he had never hugged and rocked me. Murmuring and crying, he said to her motionless body, "It's all right, baby. Stuart is here. Everything is going to be all right."

26

I did not comprehend the moment. Was time was rushing forward or standing still? All reason had disappeared. And what was that ringing in my ears? Was an insistent someone pressing a doorbell? I flinched as the repeated sol-do joined other sounds in the noisy house: rain beating against glass; Stuart moaning over Giselle; my teeth chattering like trick dice; and now, a doorbell going off. My surroundings had turned into a film noire sequence with no dialogue, just ear-assaulting noise. And then the bell went silent, its shrillness replaced by footfalls pounding through the foyer toward the horror show in the living room. The clomping was too loud to be made by one intruder. Had a police tactical team gotten wind a crime in progress? Not a shooting, though. A kidnapping. Surely, the officers would consider the crime of stealing children more heinous than…

In my compromised brain, I still thought I was the victim, not the perpetrator, and I felt certain that an attempted kidnapping would be of more interest to astute policemen than an accidental shooting. Oh, hello, officers. I'm so glad you finally got here. The man on the floor over there, do you see him, the one with the dead woman? Hurry, you must arrest him immediately. He's trying to steal my children.

But the footfalls were not police boots. A familiar voice called out my name, a female voice I recognized with utter gratitude. Oh, oh, oh, thank goodness. Rennie is here. She'll know what to do.

I did not question by what magic my old friend had caught up with me in the living room of Giselle's parents' home…in Florida… in a rain and windstorm…in the middle of the night. Imitations of reality had become commonplace to my muddled mind. (Beam me up, Scottie. Or better still…Click your heels three times and whisper, "There's no place like home.")

Rennie rushed into the living room through the archway from the hall. When I turned and beheld her beautiful face, my heart thumped an extra beat for gladness. What joy! All is not lost! Rennie will take care of everything!

"Arlena…darling," my dear rescuer said. "What happened? Are you okay?"

I did not answer. I could not. My vocal cords had gone stiff the instant the gunshot rang out. Rennie did not speak as she processed the room: Stuart and Giselle on the floor; Stuart distraught; Giselle still as death in his arms.

Then out of nowhere, Hal's face appeared over Rennie's shoulder. For a second, she appeared to have two heads. I was addled to the point of being glad to see Hal too. Strange how it slipped my mind he was one of the villains. Good…Hal is here…helpful Hal. He'll wash away the blood before it ruins the rug and tile.

Hal assimilated the scene more quickly than Rennie ever could. His face froze as he stared past her at the aftermath of the shooting. I puzzled over his sickened expression, for by then, nothing of it seemed ghastly to me, a bit out of the ordinary, perhaps, but not ghastly. I'd shot Giselle; Stuart had tried to help her; and then Rennie had come in, followed by Hal. I would not have found it odd if the angel Gabriel had shown up. Fear not, everybody. Gabriel is here. He'll tell us how to deal with all this unpleasantness.

When Stuart saw Hal, he became mobile again. He let go of Giselle's shoulders, crawled across the floor to the gun, scooped it from under the skirt of the wingback, and sprang upright. And then, as a final power stroke, he pointed the gun at the rest of us - Rennie, Hal, and me.

The seriousness of the situation had grown vague in my sluggish mind, but not in the minds of Rennie and Hal. Neither spoke a word as seconds ticked off. Stuart kept his poise; Rennie and Hal kept theirs; and since I had no poise to keep, I remained a life-sized, stringy-haired Barbie doll whose painted-on smile had long since worn off and whose ability to remain standing depended on being propped up by a chair. And though four of us were still left alive in the room, not one could have guessed the outcome of the bizarre events that followed.

27

Seconds after Stuart got his hands on the gun, the irresponsible, happy-go-lucky, never-take-anything-seriously Rennie became a military general spurring Hal and me to move. Stuart, she did not bother with. He was on his own with a firearm and a question: Shoot us or let us go?

Rennie was betting he would choose the latter. By will alone, she relocated her small company – Hal, herself, and me – from the interior of the house back to the rain-and-wind-punished driveway. Stuart made no move to stop us. He could have. He was the only one with real power. No one else was armed. But he never left the posh living room. Rennie did not linger to analyze his lack of action…whether he might be more afraid of us than we were of him or perhaps already planning the terrible deed he committed after our departure. She had no way of knowing what he was thinking, only what was in her own mind, a certain knowledge that she had to get Hal, me, and herself out of there.

Hal obeyed Rennie with no hesitation when she gestured toward me and then the foyer. He ran to my side, grabbed my hand, and dragged me in quick-step toward the front door. Rennie was close behind us when we burst outside, where slanting rain blasted our faces and soaked our hair and clothing. Too bad it could not wash away our filth. More than twenty-four hours had passed since any of us had bathed. We reeked, especially me…the insane, homicidal ex-wife who still had traces of gunpowder in the creases of her palms.

The going was slower than it should have been as we lumbered through the rain toward Rennie's BMW. I had to be helped along by my two companions. Hal bore my weight as Rennie talked me through the process of putting one foot in front of the other. I did not realize it at the time, but the passage from the death house to the sanctuary of Rennie's car – a passage I could never have traversed on my own – would be the genesis of an astonishing journey initiated by two self-less individuals willing to risk everything to save another. All my life, I had bought into the anemic sort of love represented by heart-shaped boxes of Valentine chocolates. I did not know this was no more than a cheap imitation of love, or that the real thing would manifest in my life unexpectedly in the form of two human rescuers made physically ugly by rain-streaked, distorted faces. Their odor alone on that miserable night would have repelled any seeker of romance.

Rennie's BMW proved a bless-ed haven for fugitives seeking shelter from a near-hurricane. It did not matter that its interior smelled of sour carpet and stale coffee. Rennie seldom if ever remembered to put up her windows when she parked outdoors. Lowcountry afternoon thunderstorms regularly drenched and re-drenched the seats and floorboards of her expensive rental vehicle. Add in the smell of ancient cigarette butts and vanilla air freshener discs, and you had quite the bouquet.

Rennie is such a pig, I thought, my nose tingling from the stink of the vehicle. But then I remembered my own latest sin and pulled myself up short. Up to that night, sitting in judgment of others was my most satisfying and entrenched habit. Incredibly, it took killing a person by my own hand, with a gun and a heart full of hate to break me of this unkind practice. Don't get me wrong. I would never recommend committing a grisly crime as a treatment for any sort of dysfunction. I still have trouble believing I had to experience the shock of a muzzle flash from the end of a .38 to make me see the truth, that I was the one who should have been judged all along. As I sat in the grubbiness of Rennie's vehicle, with rainwater tracking the windshield and tears tracking my cheeks, I saw in a flash of insight how superior it was to be an ordinary pig (like Rennie) whose worst sin was keeping a dirty car than a guilt-ridden murderess (like me) whose worst sin was firing a gun…lethally.

Rennie was not interested in my opinion of her unkempt vehicle, not when dealing with the practical matter of driving in a downpour. While she was preoccupied with easing the car onto Palmer Avenue, I stole a last look at the house. Turning to peer out the passenger window was a simple move, though it showcased the peculiar slowness that would characterize my every action for weeks and months to come. I stared at the closed front door. How false the look of security it suggested through the blur of sheeting rain. Deception, I thought. Utter, utter deception, that tasteful arched entrance, so picturesque, so pleasing. Miniatures of it could be cast in iron, painted artfully, and sold in ten-count cases to gift shops all over Florida. Greedy tourists on the hunt for overpriced souvenirs would snap them up in multiples to take back home to Iowa and Kansas. They'd view them as sophisticated reminiscences of the Sunshine State's stylish Spanish architecture. But then, as most dreams do, the classic Florida house-and-home of the Bordeaus receded into the distance, shrinking smaller and smaller in my vision, though not in significance to my soul, as the BMW crawled away.

I wondered with idle interest what had become of Hal, why he had not joined Rennie and me in her car. Though I did not care except in passing. Shock had distorted my connection to reality to the point that ghosts could have carried on a dinner party in my peripheral vision without it seeming peculiar.

Rennie kept the BMW's powerful engine in check as we fled the affluent neighborhood. I did not ask why she was driving so slowly. I didn't care about that, either. We were miles up the Interstate by the time I remembered we had left the Explorer behind. With the help of halting mental pondering, I reckoned that Hal must be driving it. Yes, Hal was following Rennie and me in the Explorer... oh.

And that was my last rational thought for the night. I have hazy memories of Rennie keeping up a steady string of nervous chatter once she got us safely onto the Interstate, though she could have been speaking Greek for all I understood. It was abnormal the effect her near hysteria had on me. You would have thought I might do something wild to escape it, like clamping a hand over her mouth, or jumping out of the car, or screaming my lungs out. But instead, I dropped my chin to my chest and fell asleep.

The next thing I knew, Rennie and Hal were pulling me out of the car through the passenger door, patting my cheeks and hands, calling my name. I groaned and resisted, but they refused to give in. I opened my eyes to their blurred faces bobbing up and down in my personal space. "Leave me alone," I whined. "I'm sleeping."

But Rennie was determined. "Don't close your eyes again," she said with no pity. "We're moving you to the Explorer. Hal has to get you ready for school. Open your eyes, Arly...cooperate. I have to go to Sullivan's in case anyone from Florida calls on the cottage landline."

Rennie sounded fearful, inspiring fear in me. So much that I began cooperating with Hal, though my eyes remained two swollen slits. My rescuers had difficulty transferring me from the BMW to the Explorer. I helped little as they pulled me along like an old sot who had drunk herself senseless again and could not walk alone. It was not until they crammed me into the backseat of my own vehicle – I recognized it by the improved smell – that I widened my right eye ever so slightly to see Rennie's backside through the front windshield bouncing up the sidewalk on her two chunky legs. She was running. Then she was opening the door to the BMW, jumping inside, and driving away amidst the roar of its powerful German engine.

Hal did not seem to notice she had left. He was too busy trying to wake me up. I countered his efforts by moaning about my troubles. "Where are Raven and Constantia? What am I going to do? I shot Giselle. I did. I shot her."

Hal snatched his t-shirt off and soaked a sleeve with water from a half-empty bottle he had found in the console. I protested with grunts when he grabbed my chin and tilted my head back. "Pull yourself together," he said, scrubbing at my face and hands. He had never spoken to me that way before. I did not like it and began moaning louder. He cut me off with sharp words. "Stop it, lady. You have to go in that school building in a few minutes and put up a decent front, like you were in town all night, never went to Florida."

Insulted by his impatience, I forced myself alert. "I'm not going anywhere. I'm going to...throw up."

"No, you're going to breathe in through your nose and out through your mouth, slowly... like this, slow-ly."

I don't know why I went along. It must have been the calming effect of his breathing and talking. Within seconds, I got lost in the process of in-through-your-nose-and-out-through-your-mouth, and I stopped complaining.

Hal kept up breathing slow-ly as he worked on my appearance, which, if his expression were any indication, had to be pathetic. Snatching the scrunchy off my ponytail, he began combing his fingers through the mass of tangles my hair had gotten into on the road trip. It hurt, but I did not care. I was still breathing...slow-ly. The thing was, I felt secure in his hands. Hal showed extraordinary skill at managing my long locks, his own mane being longer. In half a minute, he had worked my tangles into a bun at the nape of my neck and secured it with the scrunchy.

"I've been wanting to try your hair in a cool messy bun like this since the first day I laid eyes on you," he said, "a heck of a time to get my wish." Then he took hold of my chin again and jerked my head left and right to examine my face from different angles. I knew by his frown he was displeased.

"Hair okay," he said. "Face, not so much. Nothing to be done about it...no time for makeup. Let me straighten your shirt. It looks like you slept in it."

"I did sleep in it, and I shot Giselle in it, and now I want to burn it."

"You aren't the first teacher who slept in her clothes and went to school without changing. I've seen that un-cool move executed more than once with my own eyes...a couple of old relationships. Nothing I can do about those black smudges on your collar. When you go inside, put some marker streaks on the rest of your clothes like you got messed up doing an art project in your classroom or something. Just act normal. Don't call attention to yourself. You smell like a pole cat, but no one will notice after you mix in with those funky kids."

"I never knew you could talk so much," I said. He was scrubbing at my palms again. "I think I hate it…your talking so much."

He smirked. "What about you, the sphinx? Anyway, Rennie does enough talking for the both of us." He gave my right palm a last swipe. "Go to the restroom when you get inside – I know you need to – and while you're in there, wash your hands with soap. And grab a couple of sodas from a vending machine or steal one out of the fridge in the break room. Here, put these quarters in your pocket. You'll never get through this without caffeine."

I realized in a brain flare Hal was preparing me for hostile territory, a veritable combat zone…student teaching. "You can't make me do any of that," I said. "I have to call Stuart, find out where he's hiding Raven and Constantia. And I have to figure out what to do about Giselle."

"No, no, and no. You're going in that building and act like nothing happened. Otherwise, you'll be arrested for murder… again…only this time it'll be for real. You actually killed somebody, by accident, I hope. But believe me, she's just as dead."

"How did you find out about that other thing? It was a long time ago."

"Rennie told me. She said you were a folk hero around here for a while, blew the whistle on some criminals downtown."

"Where is Rennie now? Where did she go?"

"Sullivan's…she's trying to get there in time to catch any phone calls from Florida. Her plan is to say you were home with us all night, then got up and went to school early to get your materials ready for class. She wants to take any bad messages herself. Thinks it would be less suspicious. You know, for her to take some random call instead of you, if she can make it back to the cottage in time. Highway patrol didn't mess with us on the road, which means Stuart didn't call the police and rat us out, not yet anyway. What you've got to understand is that Rennie and I put our asses on the line bringing you back here. And now your part is going in that school this morning and behaving yourself."

"I can't."

Hal pulled his damp t-shirt back on and moved to the driver's seat. He started the engine and merged into the school lane like a veteran parent. "You can, and you will, and not just for Raven and Constantia...for Rennie and me and yourself."

I was in no shape to follow all his reasoning yet, though I complied with his demands when he succeeded in connecting in my mind that for now, taking care of a roomful of other people's children was the only way I could take care of my own. I had to save them, from what exactly, I did not I know. But save them, I must. I stopped arguing with Hal, hauled myself out of the backseat of the Explorer, and walked like a straw woman toward the school entrance.

Morning routine at Wellington was in full swing. Children loaded down with heavy backpacks shuffled along the sidewalk; vehicles waited curbside to drop other kids off at the car-rider entrance; Mrs. Hardy, the principal, officiated in four different sites at once. I turned back for a last look at Hal, imploring him with my eyes to help me find an easier way. Couldn't he see I was about to collapse? He made eye contact, said nothing, nodded encouragement. I gave up. There was nothing left to do but get on with whatever torment awaited me inside the building, all because Hal had convinced me it was necessary to suffer through to keep my children safe.

28

I had been with my students less than two hours when the principal, Mrs. Hardy, and the guidance counselor, Miss Powell, appeared at my classroom door and called me into the hallway. The grayness of their faces frightened me. Mrs. Hardy kept referring to me as dear, something she had never done before. "You're needed in the office, dear. Your friend, Reynolds, is here to tell you something, dear. You're going to have to be strong. We're family here at Wellington. We'll help any way we can...dear."

"My children...Raven and Constantia?"

"No, no," said Mrs. Hardy. "I'm so sorry. I should have made that clear first thing. They're fine. It's your ex-husband in Florida where they're visiting. Please, it'll be better if your friend explains. I'll walk with you."

She took my arm and guided me the short distance to the entrance of her office near the reception area. "Close the door if you need privacy. Take as long as you need. I'll be in the reception area."

I inhaled to subdue my dread and walked into Mrs. Hardy's office. "Rennie?" I said when I saw my pale friend occupying a visitor's chair. She looked like Rennie, but not the real Rennie. Where were her giggles, her sparkle?

She pointed toward the door. I pulled it closed behind me without taking my eyes off her pale face. I had seen my old friend tired before, but never like this, not even the night of the party calamity. No makeup, no hair gel, and was that body odor I was picking up? When the door clicked shut, she rushed toward me and grabbed my shoulders. I staggered. I was still a straw woman.

"It's worse," she said, "than even last night."

My muscles began trembling in a familiar pattern. "Raven and Constantia?"

"No, it's Stuart. He's dead. Shot himself after we left."

I slumped forward, unable to compute what she was saying. She pushed me back upright and continued. "The phone was ringing when I got back to the cottage. I caught it, barely." Pause. "Arlena, are you okay? Are you going to faint?"

I did feel faint. An invisible weight had compressed my lower vertebrae forcing me down and down. Rennie slid a chair behind me and helped me into it. She dropped to her knees in front of me and began whispering.

"We have to get you out of here. Mrs. Hardy isn't expecting you back for a few days. I told her you…we…have to go to Florida to pick up Raven and Constantia. You did right, though, coming in this morning. Hal said you were a good soldier. He's waiting outside in the Explorer. Been there the whole time in case you folded. Come on, get up…easy does it. And don't overdo the emotion in front of the office staff. Stuart was your ex, not your current."

I did not resist Rennie as she ushered me through reception where a bevy of distressed women touched my arms and shoulders and told me how sorry they were about my problem. Weak and dizzy, I focused on the floor and remained mute. The quarters Hal had given me were still in my pocket. I hadn't bought a soda. I hadn't had as much as a drink of water. Downhill was where I was heading.

Mrs. Hardy and Rennie walked me toward the exit, each holding a forearm. Hal had moved the Explorer to the fire lane a few steps from the children's entrance. He ran to meet us as we zigzagged down the walkway. Taking my weight over from the two women, he swung me up into his arms. And that was it. I was done. I have no recollection of being placed in the Explorer, or the ride back to Sullivan's, or being carried up the cottage stairs, or put to bed in my own room.

I do remember the sting of smelling salts. I could not say why in the world Rennie would have an oddball thing like smelling salts in her makeup caboodle. I only remember slapping her hand away when she stuck the bottle under my nose. "Stop," I said and bolted upright. The dreadfulness of what Rennie had told me in Mrs. Hardy's office had injured me deeply. "Oh, no, not Stuart," I cried out on waking. "He can't be dead. I just saw him, just talked to him."

Rennie and Hal exchanged looks. I pulled hard on Rennie's arm and demanded details. She got in bed beside me and held my hand as she went over what she knew. Giselle's father had called the cottage. He had told Rennie through his tears that the maid had found Giselle and Stuart in the house when she arrived at work, both of them shot dead.

Rennie squeezed my hands tighter to counteract my shuddering. This time it was grief making me tremble, not anger. Grief for my and Stuart's woeful history. And more grief for Raven and Constantia. I was not much older than they when my own parents died in Australia. It broke my heart to think of my little girls standing in the same line of suffering I had always occupied.

Rennie held me until her arms cramped though I begged her not to let go. "We have to get up," she said. "Raven and Constantia are with Giselle's mother and father. The man was a wreck on the phone. Sounded like he was a hundred years old. And I could hear his wife wailing in the background. We have to get the girls out of that environment."

I pulled away and wiped my eyes with the backs of my hands. "Yes, yes, we have to go to the airport. It'll be quicker to fly. What about reservations, tickets, lead time?"

Rennie stroked my hand. "Hal is taking care of everything. He's on the phone in the kitchen. I've asked him to go with us. We need his help."

"You wouldn't say that if you knew what he's been doing."

"I do know…now. He told me everything on the road to Florida when we were on our way to find you. And he's sorry, Arlena… sincerely, he is. I have to believe him after the risk he took helping me get you home. I couldn't have done it without him, not with your car in Winter Park, and the shape you were in when we got there. Bringing you back had to be some kind of crime. Hal and I would be charged with I-don't-know-what if the police found out we transported you across state lines. Accessory to murder? Something after the fact? I'm scared just thinking about it. And now you have to let him help us again. I can't do this by myself. It's too much. I haven't even had time to call Texas to tell Clark about Stuart and Giselle."

"Everything is so messed up, Rennie. I'm sick. I can't deal with Hal, not even if you're on his side. He's been helping Stuart and Giselle for money."

Rennie did not give in to my drama. "Florida is going to be intense," she said. "Giselle's parents are flattened. Stuart's will be, too. You know they'll fly straight down there if they're able. And the police…by now, they're investigating. It'll be chaos in every direction. We have to nail down a story, an alibi. Hal and I are prepared to swear to whatever."

"But why would you do that? Why would Hal?"

"I'm your best friend, your only friend from what I've seen since I've been here. And I'm not going to stand by and let the legal system take you away from your girls, lock you up. People get pushed into things. You didn't mean to kill Giselle. And you didn't mean for Stuart to kill himself. Raven and Constantia need their mother, and if I have my way, they're going to have her. As for Hal, the poor guy is convinced the whole thing is his fault beginning to end. He's dying of remorse, working his fingers to the bone trying to turn things around. We have no choice but to let him help us. We need him."

"I want to go to the authorities right away. They'll understand how everything happened once I explain."

"Out of the question. You drove six hundred miles one way with a gun and bullets in your vehicle, all the way from South

Carolina to dang Florida. If that doesn't scream premeditation, I don't know what does."

"How did you know I had the gun?"

"Hal knew when he couldn't find it in his footlocker. I'm telling you, the boy freaked."

"I'm still not talking to him," I said.

"You're stuck on the wrong thing, Arly. Forget being mad at Hal. We have to cook up a story. Get down off your high horse and do what's best for your children. Every move you make from now on has got to be for them. You're their mother. It's your responsibility to protect their future."

"I don't know how. I can't think."

"How about I slap you to clear your mind. This ain't the movies. Go the bathroom and get cleaned up. You stink."

29

After my shower, Rennie sat with me while I picked at a grilled cheese sandwich and sipped from a mug of canned chicken soup. When she saw how much trouble I was having getting anything down, she brought me a tumbler of iced ginger ale, which helped my sick stomach but not the detached sensation that had settled over me.

I was able to absorb in part what Rennie was telling me. And I wanted to cooperate. I did, honestly. But my mind had dulled to the point that not much was getting through. The only good thing was that I realized my own incapacitation. I knew I had no alternative but to let Rennie do my thinking for me, right or wrong, smart or dumb. Though even to a jumbled brain like mine, Rennie's conviction that we could not get by without the help of a known betrayer (Hal) seemed more than off base. It seemed insane.

⌘ ⌘ ⌘

In Florida we encountered a cacophony of talk, questions, suppositions, weeping, gnashing of teeth, and rampant confusion. Moments after we arrived at the Bordeaus' condominium – Rennie had called ahead and arranged a time for us to pick up Raven and Constantia – I became ill with remorse. I was in no way prepared for the depth of grief I had inflicted upon Giselle's parents. Their only child was dead; I had been the cause; and now I wished I were dead too.

On entering the old couple's new world of despair, Rennie became a woman possessed. She took one look at them - bent father and traumatized mother - and concluded correctly that Raven and Constantia were in an unhealthy situation. But despite her best efforts at speeding up the process of freeing them, she found herself mired in the sheer misery of the wounded old people. Mrs. Bordeau's pain was all consuming. I suffered along with her each time she dissolved into tears on trying to speak. Her husband's condition was worse. He who had been bled dry himself was spending the last vestiges of his strength trying to console his distraught wife. As I witnessed their agony, the weight of my remorse became unbearable. I thought I would surely suffocate.

Rennie's insistence on Hal coming with us made sense now. So did her plan to remove Raven and Constantia from the home of Giselle's parents as quickly as possible and assume care of them herself. Hal's job was to mind me as far as I would let him. Every now and then I found the strength to resist. Those were the times Rennie would step in and break things down for me in practical terms: "Choose your poison: me watching after the twins, and Hal watching after you, or the other way around."

Which was no choice at all. As much as I hated to admit it, I did need watching after. The sight of Giselle's parents had pierced my heart to the core and set my conscience aflame. Their distorted faces appeared scorched, as if they'd been too near an explosion and barely escaped being burned alive. It was excruciating to confront the awful damage caused by my misdeed with a deadly handgun. I had been too busy feeding my own rationalizations to realize the enormity of my selfish act, convincing myself that Giselle was no more than a caricature of a one-dimensional, artificial, narcissistic, spoiled woman. But when I saw her grieving parents, a different perception came thundering to the forefront of my mind. Giselle was a real person, the only child of two failing old people who loved her as much as any other parents love their children...including me as a parent. And now their precious Giselle was gone from their lives, and Raven and Constantia would be gone soon, taking with them the Bordeaus' last hope for grandchildren. The sadness on their gray faces told a terrible story. They had lost their only child, and now they were terrified that Raven and Constantia's biological mother, me, would swoop in and take them away as well to the sure purpose of severing all contact. No more Giselle. No more sweet little ones. No more reason to live.

30

Relief flooded my soul when I saw my children. They ran to me the moment I stepped through the entryway of the Bordeau dwelling. I cannot describe to you the humble gratitude I felt as they wrapped their slender arms around my legs. I thought I had lost them, and now I had them back. What can I say to make you understand the anguish of such a thing...the panic, terror, utter desperation of thinking my children had been stolen, followed by the unexpected joy and relief of reuniting with them? How can I make you feel the intensity of that phantasmagoria of emotions?

I loved Raven and Constantia more than life itself in that moment of reconnection, yet I had little in the way of comfort to offer them and less in the way of protection. I was too feeble to lift them out of the pit into which I had let them fall. It was a perilous crater inhabited by ravenous adults, the very ones on whom they had depended for their safety. My worst fear was that somewhere deep in their souls they knew I had let them down. What a living nightmare. Who can innocent babes count on if not their mother?

I wanted to hold my twins close forever in that doorway to the Bordeaus' stylish condo, but dizziness overtook me. Hal held me steady as Rennie peeled the girls off my legs and transferred them to herself. I heard their muffled sobs. And if I had not known them so well, I might have thought they were crying for Stuart and Giselle. But they were not old enough for that. They were crying from fatigue and confusion at being snatched out of the condo swimming pool by a near stranger. For Stuart had been telling the truth about where they were the night of the gun. Giselle's mother and father had invited them for a sleep-over at their condominium, doable even at their advanced age due to the help provided by a young French au pair hired by Giselle the week before. The inexperienced nanny had been whimpering as she shepherded the dripping twins from pool to elevator to condo, which frightened them so much they began whimpering along with her without knowing why, and they had been crying off and on ever since.

Rennie lifted Constantia to her hip and held Raven close by her hand. Hal had all he could do to deal with me. "Stop blocking my way," I kept demanding. "I have to talk to Giselle's parents, make them understand."

But he never wavered in his resolve to protect me from myself. Nor did Rennie. "Keep her walking," she said to Hal about me. "Get her back to the car. She doesn't know what she's doing."

And he did get me back to the car when all I wanted was to make my way deeper into the condo and stop the pain I had caused two elderly strangers. I needed to recount to them the details surrounding their daughter's death, then go straight to the authorities to underscore how sorry I was for my part in it. Didn't I owe that much to those two broken old people whose lives I had shattered? And though I had not seen Stuart's mother and father since the disaster, didn't I owe the same to them? I wanted someone, anyone, to punish me, not forgive me.

"Rennie, Rennie, you're wrong," I said after Hal got through squashing his four passengers into the back seat of our rented Altima. The scramble of getting settled had resulted in Constantia being wedged between Rennie and me, and Raven perched on Rennie's lap. No child was in a car seat, no adult in a seatbelt. But in spite of being squeezed inside the vehicle with zero hope of escape, I kept up my inappropriate declarations.

"I can't go on like this. You have to let me tell everyone what happened...Giselle's parents...and Stuart's parents when they get here. It's dreadful what I've done to these people."

Rennie leaned over Constantia and Raven and got in my face nose to nose. "Stop talking like that in front of you-know-who," she said. "Grow a brain."

By this time, Hal had taken control of the steering wheel was now negotiating the turn out of the parking area. But when he caught the gist of what I was saying to Rennie, he hit the brakes, causing all four of us in the backseat to lurch forward. Raven landed on Rennie's feet on the floorboard. Which did not appear to concern Hal at all. It was my loose talk that had gotten his attention. He swiveled his torso around to assess what new manner of madness I was spewing out.

After the jolt of the stop, Rennie was first to get organized enough to speak. "Dammit to hell, Arlena," she said, still in the process of getting Raven off the floor and back into her lap. "I'll strangle you right here in this stinking rental car if you open your mouth one more time."

Raven looked up at her and grinned. "You said a bad word, Aunt Rennie. Two bad words."

"Oh, yeah?" Rennie said and pinched the child's ear. "If you listen hard, you might hear me say more." Then she shouted for Hal to drive.

"Dammit to hell," Raven whispered and waited for Rennie's outraged response. But Rennie just raised her eyebrows in fake shock. "Don't say that again," she whispered to Raven. "Or I'll have to spank you with a mushy spaghetti noodle."

I also admonished my child, but more forthrightly. "Behave yourself, Raven. Put your head on Rennie's shoulder and be quiet like your sister."

Raven stuck her thumb in her mouth like her sister and rooted a nesting place for her blond head upon Rennie's plump bosom, though careful to position herself so that she could continue staring at me in defiance.

I ignored her and spoke to Rennie again. "I'm right about this," I said. "I have to tell someone."

Rennie glared anger at me. "Not an option," she said. Then holding Raven's little body tight against her chest, she leaned forward and thumped Hal's shoulder. "Help me," she said. "I'm dying back here."

Hal, having given up all hope of straightening out the insanity in the back seat, refused eye contact with any of us, including Rennie. "You're right," he said to the steering wheel. Rennie thumped him again. "Stop it," Hal said to her. "You don't have to convince me. I know we can't pull this off unless we stick together. But we have to talk later. There's a corn field in here."

Raven pulled her thumb out of her mouth with a wet pop. "Talk now," she said. "I want to hear."

Rennie gave me a look. I was not deterred. In a whisper, I said to her, "You know I'm right."

Rennie did not bother to whisper back. She shouted in her most forceful voice, "If you don't stop talking crap, Arlena, I'll rent a separate car to keep you away from these children. So help me, I will."

Her fierceness shut me up for the time being, but it did not alter my thinking. I knew what I had to do. Rennie interpreted my silence as surrender. Softening her tone, she said to Raven and Constantia, "I'm sorry, darlings. Aunt Rennie didn't mean to shout. And never, ever let me hear either of you say crap. It's a bad word. How about some ice cream later to make everything all better?"

The girls nodded in an unsure manner. Raven crawled from Rennie's lap to mine and snuggled in sideways. I put my right arm around her and my left arm around her sister. "Yes, ice cream," I said. "See how much Aunt Rennie loves you. She's going to get your favorite treat. But only if you rest a few minutes. Aunt Rennie wants to tell you a story…Goldilocks."

Rennie's voice droning the details of the fairy tale was all it took to entrance the tired little girls. They were sound asleep before the bears returned to the cottage.

31

We drove to a hotel on the outskirts of Winter Park and checked into three rooms, two of them connecting. At first the desk clerk assured us no more adjoining rooms were available, but when Rennie made moves to leave, this same clerk began tapping her keyboard again and found exactly what we needed. A-mazing.

Once Rennie had gotten us locked safely inside our rooms, she pronounced that my talk of confessing had proven me untrustworthy, and she was not letting me out of her sight ever again. "You've gone nuts," she said, "temporarily I hope, but for now, crazy as a bat."

She did not belabor the point, just went about installing Raven and Constantia in one of the connecting rooms and herself and me in the other. Hal was on his own in the single, though as it turned out, he didn't sleep in it. He said he was too jittery from the ordeal at the Bordeaus and did not feel comfortable being isolated in case he was needed. But it wasn't really the Bordeaus making him nervous. It was I. When he told Rennie there was no way he could protect us if we were separated, she did not argue. The third room stood empty.

I had no vision of what I should or should not be doing. The deadening mechanism in my brain had kicked in again rendering me unable to recognize the gravity of my…our…situation. Like Nero playing his violin while Rome burned, I tucked myself into bed with Raven and Constantia and read story after story to them from the collection of picture books Rennie had brought along from Sullivan's Island. The trials of Hansel and Gretel contending with a witch in the business of cannibalism – Let me feel your finger, my dear, to see if you've grown fatter – seemed comforting next to the problems of real life.

For an hour I read to my girls like a faithful loving mom, while Hal watched (guarded) us from an armchair across the room. He appeared to be as intent as the twins upon learning the fate of Hansel and Gretel. I read using a witchy voice or children's voices at appropriate times. This, my tired mind assured me, was the top priority for the time being…drawing comfort from my children and allowing my children to draw comfort from me. I suppressed for that short interlude the gruesome details of bullets piercing flesh, intended or unintended. Let the bad memories sneak up later in night terrors, I thought. Or better still, let them be repressed and forgotten altogether.

Though my disassociation was now operating at an alarming level, I was still able to hear Rennie making phone calls in the next room. Her anger at me had somehow transformed her personality from scatterbrain to over-achiever. I understood that the calls had to do with my problems, not hers, and she was taking my burdens onto her own shoulders. I also knew I should feel grateful, but I did not. I felt resentful. I was the dependable one, not Rennie. Everyone who knew us in college joked about this imbalance in our relationship. I took care of Rennie. Rennie did not take care of me. I attended classes faithfully and completed my work. Rennie specialized in cutting classes and eschewing all assignments except jazzy art projects. I avoided alcohol, late hours, and sleeping around. Rennie embraced all three. I was her keeper, a dynamic in our relationship apparent to everyone. It was a convenience enjoyed by Rennie. It helped keep her parents at bay, the two unsuspecting innocents to whom I told more lies over the four years Rennie and I were roommates than I have told collectively in my entire life, all to keep them in the dark about their daughter's bad habits and questionable whereabouts.

I pondered how two shootings in Florida had somehow turned my and Rennie's relationship upside down. Or perhaps it had taken events that horrific to turn it right side up. After all, Rennie was not a murderess like me, just a mere rounder...tame by comparison.

Her phone calls from the other room were too numerous to track. Someone, Stuart's parents, I think, had made arrangements for a memorial service. They must have put plans into motion by telephone before leaving Boston, after receiving the heartbreaking news from Giselle's father. Rennie found out by calling around that the Princes and Bordeaus had decided to cremate their children's bodies and bury their ashes together in a local cemetery. But since forensic autopsies had to be performed as required by Florida police investigations involving deaths by gunshot, the two sets of grieving parents felt the need to go ahead and have a memorial service sans bodies in the chapel of a Winter Park funeral home. While still reading to Raven and Constantia, I heard Rennie tell Hal to call the place every hour or so to check for details concerning arrangements. I did not have the presence of mind to feel relief that I, Stuart's ex-wife, had no responsibility to plan such things.

The trickiest phone call was to a Detective Smythe, head of the Winter Park Police Department's investigation team for the shootings. Mr. Bordeau had given Smythe's number to Rennie on a slip of paper that also bore my name and a cryptic message from Smythe himself. Call me, please.

But when Rennie succeeded in getting him on the line, he refused to discuss anything. I was the one he wanted to talk to in person. Rennie, cell phone still in hand, looked worried when she entered the room where the rest of us had slipped into rest mode. Raven and Constantia had fallen asleep under the bed covers. Hal was snoozing in the armchair from whence he had been guarding us.

Rennie looked puzzled when she caught me staring at Hal from across the room. He was defenseless in sleep, head propped far back, legs stretched out, heels braced deep in the carpet. His closed eyes revealed dark lids and blond lashes pressed against bluish circles on the skin below. He looked as if he had two black eyes. Had he been in a fist fight I did not know about? Meanwhile, on the other side of the room, the more unreliable person (that would be me), who needed guarding due to her new ambition to turn herself in to the authorities, lay content in a cloud of her children's sweet breath.

Rennie gave me a hand signal from the doorway to rise and join her in the other bedroom. She glanced back in Hal's direction, then she walked to the armchair where he lay sleeping, not guarding anyone. She hesitated, most likely feeling sorry for him because he looked so tired – believe me, we all looked tired – before touching his shoulder to rouse him. Startled, he sprang to his feet and assumed a defensive posture. Rennie told him with her eyes to settle down and watch the girls while she and I were in the other room.

To her irritation, I took a few extra seconds to straighten Raven and Constantia's small bodies in bed and tuck them in tighter. Reluctantly, I left my children with Hal in the dim bedroom and accompanied Rennie to the brighter room next door.

"A detective…" she began as I followed her through the doorway, "…is driving over here to 'have a word with you.' How formal is that?"

My thoughts raced. The opportunity to confess was coming straight to our door. Why then did I feel like hiding in a closet? No, I thought to myself. I can't tell the truth quite yet. I'm too rattled. Better to wait a few days, keep the waters muddied a bit longer, give my mind a chance to clear.

Suddenly a different fear gripped my heart, that of getting caught in a web of lies. What had the officer already discovered? He had to have found the gun. But what else? Fibers, fingerprints, witnesses? For all I knew there were servants in the house who had seen and heard everything, who'd already given eyewitness accounts. Had it been a mistake for Rennie and Hal to snatch me away like that? Maybe this detective was on his way over to arrest all three of us for...

The hotel room began rocking worse than Giselle and Stuart's living room the night of the gun. I backed to the edge of the bed and sat down. "What do you think he wants?" I asked.

"To conduct a routine interview to 'rule you out as a suspect,' or so he said. You can't fall apart. It makes sense for you to be nervous, but not hysterical. And whatever you do, don't let him trick you. Remember our story: You spent the day of the incident studying at the cottage. And Hal and I came in later. And we were both with you the rest of the night. And then we all went to bed early to get ready for the coming school week...student teaching for you, classes for Hal and me. Keep it simple, no details that can trip you up later."

"I want to tell the truth. No, I don't want to tell the truth. But if I do, he'll see it was an accident, the part about what happened to Giselle anyway. I don't know why Stuart shot..."

My face contorted. This was Stuart I was talking about, my Stuart, who'd committed suicide with the same monstrous gun that had killed Giselle. The man I had loved in my youth. It was curious how easily my mind slipped into a distant and dishonest history. I forgot all bitterness as I conjured up nothing except my and Stuart's early lives together and how happy we had been(?). And then I began fretting again about how his death was going to affect Raven and Constantia in the future. Was it my fault he and Giselle were both dead? Of course, it was my fault. I could not unshoot a gun. Neither could Stuart.

My fresh attack of sobbing alerted Hal. He appeared in the doorway of the girls' room. He and Rennie exchanged looks again, the same kind they'd been exchanging since I first mentioned telling the truth to the police. It was apparent they had no faith in me. And here I was making it worse, working myself into another emotional state.

Their concern was no over-reaction. I had not seen a lucid moment since I discovered Stuart was trying to take Raven and Constantia, and that Giselle was helping him, and Hal too. As I sat crying my eyes out on the side of the lumpy bed in that cheap hotel room, my self-pity morphed into rage. I focused my fury on Hal now standing quietly in the doorway. On remembering the crisp, professional copies of his reports to Stuart about my unfitness as a mother, I became so angry I jumped up, still sobbing, and ran across the room to attack him. I pounded his chest with my bony fists.

"Why did you do it," I said, bashing away at him with ineffective blows. He did not defend himself. He remained immobile until I wore myself out and began a slow slide to my knees. He dropped to his own knees and held me as my tantrum played out, the last of it consisting of nothing but powerless verbal assaults. "I don't understand. How could you? You were helping Stuart the whole time."

And for the first time, Hal cried too. Or maybe not for the first time. Maybe he had been crying alone or on Rennie's shoulder since Florida. I became aware of his body trembling as I leaned on him for support, yet I felt no sympathy. His broken phrases scraped against my eardrums like metal on metal. "I don't know," he said. "Money, stupidity. But you have to believe how sorry I am. It's all my fault; I caused everything. And I'm going to help you get through this...out of this. I'm going to help you if it takes the rest of my life."

The sound of his voice sickened me. "You're sorry all right," I said, "a sorry human being."

Rennie ran into the bathroom and turned on the sink taps full force. "You're driving me nuts, the both of you," she called out, her words amplified by the tile walls. "That viper detective is on his way over here to grill us, and the two of you are acting like idiots."

She marched back into the bedroom carrying a wet hand towel. "I can't take it anymore," she said as Hal maneuvered me into a chair and positioned me so that Rennie could wash my face. "Straighten up, Arlena. Am I the only one around here thinking of Raven and Constantia? I don't want to hear any more of your brand of truth. Truth is overrated. Do you hear me? Overrated! Hold still...let me wipe the snot off your face. You look like death. Hal, go wash your own face. Why do I have to be every-freakin'-body's mother?"

32

Minutes before Detective Smythe arrived, Hal left our connected rooms to hide out in the unconnected single. Rennie said it would be better if she and I met with the detective by ourselves. Her logic was that a police officer might not feel as aggressive talking to two women by themselves. Said she, "We need every edge we can get."

When the knock came, I remained in my chair as Rennie answered the door to a tall trim man with gray hair, gray mustache, and dark complexion. He wore street clothes and a tight neat shoulder holster encasing a black-handled handgun. I looked at it and wondered why anyone would want to have to do with such an instrument of violence. Then I remembered, I myself had had to do with one not very long ago. As I stared at the revolver's black grip, I recalled reading somewhere that statistically most policemen don't have to point their guns at anyone over their entire careers, much less shoot. And I had done both in one evening.

Rennie ushered the officer into the room. He looked around automatically, professionally, efficiently, then he took a seat in the desk chair offered to him by Rennie, his cheery hostess. Before he arrived, cheery hostess had placed un-cheery me in one of the matching leatherette armchairs. She now took a seat in the other and waited for the newest misery to begin. I, like a hapless patient about to be evaluated by a psychiatrist with the ultimate intention of committing her to an insane asylum, remained on the edge of my seat leaving nothing to support my back. Every inch of my body ached, had been aching for days. I suppressed my pain by focusing on the detective's face, though still aware of the cold hard stare Rennie was boring into my profile. Her purpose was to will me to behave. She was determined to stop me from giving in to guilt, saying something stupid, forgetting my responsibilities to Raven and Constantia. No way was she going to let me succumb to the perverted belief that the criminal justice system would forgive my sins if only I'd confess them to a sin-free police officer and wait for a sin-free judge in some sin-free court room to punish me so thoroughly that the evil of what I had done would be wiped away. Rennie meant to stand in the breach between me and my own unclear thinking. She was convinced I did not understand the pointlessness of my wish to be absolved. Truth be told, she remains convinced in her own nightmares to this day.

Detective Smythe was obscenely polite as are all law enforcement officials, condescending in a manner intended to intimidate and humiliate suspects and perpetrators. I knew in an instant his courtesy did not originate in his heart, but in the bile sac connected to his gall bladder. He offered condolences...to me, in particular. It appeared he did not think Rennie needed consoling. In fact, I began to wonder if he had forgotten she was in the room. He directed everything toward me alone, told me not to be alarmed, that it was customary for WPPD, Winter Park Police Department, to conduct formal investigations into all homicide cases.

"Homicide!" Rennie blurted out. "I thought you had already figured out that for some reason Stuart killed Giselle and then shot himself, murder-slash-suicide. Happens all the time. I see it on crime shows all the time." (Which was not a good reference of expertise on the subject to make her point!)

"We treat every case individually," responded the detective so respectfully I felt like slapping him. And then he promptly forgot

Rennie's presence again and trained his laser eyes back on me. I wondered if he had spotted my twitching left eyelid, or smelled my bad breath, or heard the spongy wheezing in my chest. The flood of tears I had been experiencing over the last few days had wreaked havoc on my lungs, eyes, and skin. I felt embarrassed at being half-speed in the presence of this dapper man. The more he scrutinized me, the more I withered. Even if I had not been the suspicious character I essentially was, I would have looked and felt the part.

Stop worrying, I told myself. What could he possibly know? Oh, of course...he knows everything. He's just acting as if he doesn't. He's going to sit there like a vulture and listen to me tell lie after lie, then mock me as he clamps on the cuffs.

In a motion so slow you would never consider it a natural, I closed and opened my eyes. It was the same slowness of movement that had been dogging me since the shooting. I turned and looked at Rennie, who, like Detective Smythe, was blistering me with a stare. Her face quivered with barely concealed panic as she returned my blank look. She knew beyond question I was not in control. Detective Smythe knew too. The second he laid eyes on me, his face registered awareness, as if encountering symptoms he had seen before...shakiness, unreliability, shame. His calm appraisal put me at a disadvantage. I felt like a sloppy drunk who had been plucked out of a bar and told to sit up straight and participate sensibly in a panel discussion on the theory of relativity...or else I would be shot at sunset. The detective, however, with his knife-pressed khakis and razor-sharp intellect, and let us not forget his clear conscience, appeared to be congratulating himself already on vanquishing his latest foe.

"Detective?" Rennie said. My callow best friend had no previous experience with the technique of silence used by professional interrogators to control conversations. She fell straight into Detective Smythe's hands. Her frayed nerves wanted every cubic inch of air space in the room to be filled with words and more words, hollow or not. She could not restrain herself from speaking again when he refused to respond the first time. "Sir?" she said. "You were talking about homicide."

The man had no intention of letting an unprofessional like Rennie pace his interview. As far as he was concerned, Reynolds Brentwood did not exist. He remained silent two more long seconds before dropping a piece of information that electrified the air. "There was a note, Mrs. Prince," he said. "Your ex-husband left a note."

So...I thought, this is how it's going to end, my short career of shooting guns, killing people, lying to police officers. Rennie must have thought the same, only she was not struck speechless. Her face drained of color, yes, but that did not stop her from firing more questions toward the hostile man who had already determined she was invisible. "What note?" she said. "Why would Stuart write a note?"

Detective Smythe owned the room. In truth, he'd owned it from the moment cheery hostess Rennie had answered his knock, invited him in, and offered him a seat. He was in control all right, though at first, Rennie and I had not grasped that fact. Now we did, though. The cool, calm, collected Detective Smythe had convinced us.

In his own sweet time, he addressed several issues to do with the note, issues that hung in the air like bad odors. "Main thing... it didn't make sense," he said...bored, careful, coiled. "Not to any of us on the force anyway, or family members. You've met the victims' elderly parents, right? I guess that's why we started wondering whether you might be able to make heads or tails of it, Mrs. Prince, being Mr. Prince's ex-wife and all." He cocked his head like a puppy. But he was not a puppy. He was a snake.

My jaw dropped. I had to work at responding. "Me? I...I don't know anything."

Rennie cut my stuttering short by snapping at Smythe. "What are you talking about? Is her name on the note?"

An ever so slight look of irritation passed over the detective's cold eyes. He rotated his head sideways and glared at Rennie in a manner that shouted, I wish you would go back to being invisible! "I already told you, no one's name is on the note," he snarled. The rattler in the room was no longer logy. It was alert, preparing to strike.

Satisfied he had frightened Rennie into silence, Smythe recoiled and shifted his attention back to me, his chosen prey. By then I had sunk into an abyss of terror precisely where he wanted me to be.

"Are you willing to take a look at it, Mrs. Prince? It's true, it isn't addressed to you, doesn't mention your name or anything. But it reads like a message. Coded, possibly. From my experience, suicide victims don't take the trouble to write notes unless they're trying to communicate something, usually to a particular person. It's their way of explaining why they did it...you know...kill themselves."

He removed a folded sheet from the inside breast pocket of his sport jacket and handed it to me. Rennie jumped from her chair and rushed to stand behind me. She stared at the note over my shoulder as I unfolded and read it, my left eye now twitching madly.

Scrawled in Stuart's hand in lower-case letters with no punctuation was the phrase, tower in the sky. Rennie saw no meaning in the words and declared as much forthwith. I, however, saw volumes. It was the story of my and Stuart's wasted relationship, all within the crucible of a poem by Kahlil Gibran. Detective Smythe had guessed correctly. Stuart was communicating with a person, his ex-wife.

The crumpled note trembled in my hands. With my tongue, I worried the spot on my lip that was still scabby from being chewed so savagely the night of the shooting. It was a struggle to remain calm. Again, Rennie came to my defense on pain of being bitten by the serpent occupying the desk chair. "Arlena, do you hear Raven and Contantia?" She gestured toward the closed door to their room. "They won't sleep tonight if we let them nap too long."

As always, the simple mention of my children's names, helped me connect with my surroundings. I looked at the door and listened for my girls. When no sounds were evident, I realized Rennie had not heard anything either. She was telling me to keep Raven and Constantia in the forefront of my mind and not to let an aging homicide detective throw me off.

The taste of blood from my chewed lip reminded me that the snake in the room was deadly. Meanwhile, Detective Smythe watched his grandstand play run aground, that of introducing Stuart's note into the proceedings. He jumped too quickly to save it. Though anyone could have told him it would be a mistake to get in the way of a mother listening for her children. "Does the note mean anything to you, Mrs. Prince? You seemed upset when you saw it."

He had lost control. His words were now urgent, his expression tense, his body stiff, the combination of which effectively derailed his offensive. Darling Rennie had interfered with the old pro's timing just enough to shift the power in the room. It is remarkable the difference two seconds can make.

My bold and fearless pal wasted no time snatching the reins from Smythe by issuing a disdainful request to him concerning the children. "Could you please be quiet a second? We're trying to hear if the twins are awake."

Then she made an enormous show of tip-toeing to the connecting door and pressing her ear against its cheap fake woodgrain. Detective Smythe's supremacy shrunk to nothing in the wake of this unfair move. He could not compete with the needs of little ones. Rennie showed him no mercy. "Arlena, is that Raven…or Constantia?" she said.

"Let them be," I responded with renewed confidence. "They need rest after what they've been through."

Rennie came close to smiling as she stared at me, her expression now hopeful, grateful. And this time I did not let her down. I locked eyes with Detective Smythe and thrust the note back at him. "Sorry," I said. "It makes no sense to me."

This was the finishing blow to his assault. Disappointment replaced the look of boredom in his dark eyes. He took the note and refolded it. And though he stayed another ten minutes interviewing me about the details of my movements over the past forty-eight hours, his questions did not amount to much more than eliminating me as a suspect, not pointing a finger. The value of the dialogue had gone up in smoke the moment I dismissed the note…full stop.

Detective Smythe left with no ceremony when I came down with a suspicious weak spell, resulting in his being oh-so-sorry for making my ordeal worse, or so he forced himself to say. Rennie swore with relief as she shut the door behind him. My own relief manifested in more tears. The burst of strength I had summoned from the land-of-nothing-and-nowhere evaporated as I wept anew.

Rennie led me to the bed. She lay down beside me and gathered me in her arms. We did not talk. I relaxed in the scent of her freshly shampooed hair and stopped crying as she rocked me, though my heart continued to ache over the mess I had made of everyone's lives – Raven and Constantia's, Giselle and Stuart's, their parents', maybe even Rennie and Hal's. Stuart's note injured me in ways beyond anyone else's perception. Rennie had no knowledge of the specifics behind my new tears, and I hadn't the strength to explain. But my friend, a special and empathetic Rennie whom I had never met before, did not seem to mind. Her intent was to provide me comfort while I endured an onslaught of fresh pain. She shielded me sweetly, enveloping my heart in genuine love not of the greeting card variety. I would have died of pain that week if Rennie had not shown me unconditional love, a unique gift in my experience. Yes, Raven and Constantia were able with no effort to elicit mother's love from my heart. And from that, I was able to make the transition to a broader definition of unconditional love, all because of my loyal friend, Rennie.

Hal, however, was a different story. I would like to have hated him as much as I loved Rennie, yet I found it difficult to work up the feeling. He had betrayed me in the deepest sense, a memory I wanted to keep firm in my mind. And since I had no proficiency in forgiving and did not want any, I continued feeding my rage against Hal by rehashing in my thoughts what he had done. I did not want to forgive anyone, not Hal, nor Stuart and Giselle, nor myself. It never occurred to me the act of forgiving would begin the process of my own healing. I suspect I was not ready to be healed, or maybe I didn't want to be. I craved punishment.

For the minutes of my latest crying spell, I clung to Rennie for consolation. Though it was becoming obvious even to me that if I did not stop crying, I was going to make myself ill. Thus, for the sake of Raven and Constantia, I called forth my straw woman persona again, for as everyone knows, straw women do not cry.

33

Who could have predicted that Detective Smythe's interest in Stuart's note would progress to all out obsession? His hunch that I might know what it meant was not a stretch for an experienced law enforcement officer. When anyone dies by gunshot, and foul play is suspected, a professional will always look first in the direction of the spouse and/or ex-spouse as persons of interest. Smythe was merely following protocol to start his investigation with me, to my unending discomfort.

But, as atypical as it was, the first break he got in the case came from his own family. He had a daughter who was dating a graduate student at Florida State. The young man had taken several courses in comparative religions, and when Smythe's daughter told him about the murder/suicide case her father was working on, and quoted the four-word message in the mysterious suicide note, the young man knew its exact reference in Kahlil Gibran's poem, "The Farewell," from his book, *The Prophet.*

If in the twilight of memory.
We should meet once more,
We shall speak again together,
And you shall sing to me a deeper song.
And if our hands should meet in another dream,
We shall build another tower in the sky.

All of which doused oil on the fire of Smythe's imagination. Over the next day or two, he called me multiple times to quiz me about what meaning I thought the reference from Gibran might have to the victim. He never called Stuart by name, referred to him only as the victim. I hated when he did that, and I hated worse the way he abused me over the phone concerning two fascinating theories he was developing about the fatalities. At least he considered them fascinating, though I did not. I considered them unnerving, and more so when he changed nomenclature in mid-conversation and began referring to the fatalities as homicides.

Theory One: The two gunshot victims were having marital difficulties, and Mr. Prince's dying hope was for a second chance at their happiness in the afterlife; hence, his written message was to no one, really, just an expression of a desperate man's wish for better times with his beloved wife subsequent to their departure from the physical world. Now then, if this theory divined by Smythe out of pure bat guano were correct, the series of events the police had surmised at the crime scene were accurate down to the last detail; i.e., Stuart had shot Giselle and then himself.

"But what if I'm wrong?" Smythe would then say. "What if Prince had someone other than his current wife in mind when he wrote that phrase, a current lover or old flame?"

It was this possibility that led the crafty detective to Theory Two: Stuart was having an affair. And maybe he had decided he didn't want to live any longer without his new love? And maybe she had broken up with him, maybe that very night, and he could not face the fact he'd lost her. And maybe it had all happened right before the shootings. Or maybe Stuart was the one who'd broken it off, sending the other woman into a murderous rage. Maybe she had been in the house. And most bizarre of all, maybe she was the one who had shot Giselle and then fled, after which Stuart shot

theory. Stuart was their father. They needed to experience his memorial service as a last goodbye. "For closure," she had said, "like on made-for-TV movies." Rennie could always be counted upon to connect the shallow with the deep.

But the moment we entered the chapel, I knew I should have listened to my inner voice. I really should have. What possible good could have come from Raven and Constantia hearing a series of strangers make sad speeches about Stuart and Giselle, or from attending the reception afterwards at the Bordeaus' condo home and observing gray-faced adults soothe their feelings with heavy hor d'ouvres and alcohol. Anyone in his right mind would have known better…if anyone in his right mind had been a part of this drama.

The girls were not the only ones out of place at the service. I shouldn't have been there either. I am sure my face never once lost the look of a shocked cartoon character. The entire experience was horrendous, but the biggest stunner at the reception was the huge wedding photo of Stuart and Giselle that the Bordeaus had set up on a console table. There they were, Florida's happiest newly-weds caught in the act of running hand-in-hand down a grand outdoor staircase with blurry streaks of rice flying at them from every direction. Stuart was wearing a tux with a pleated white shirt and black tie, and Giselle a formal wedding gown, designer by the look of it. They were the stylish couple in every bridal magazine photo shoot – Giselle, the ecstatic bride…Stuart, the beaming groom. Who would ever have guessed on gazing at such an idyllic image that the groom had made the very same vows to a different woman a few short years prior?

I don't know why the photo awoke a feeling of jealousy in my soul. Was there a remote possibility I hated Giselle for more than her corrupt interest in my children? Did I hate her, if only a little, for her inexplicable interest in Stuart? I reminded myself as I looked at the staged picture that I was the one who had ended my and Stuart's marriage way before Giselle had come along. I also coached myself on the reality of the photo. It was nothing more than a record of a social event made possible by Giselle's family money. It pained me to realize I had been a party to Raven and Constantia being exposed to that kind of in-your-face propaganda for weeks on end, the popular notion that wealth can buy happiness. I had not fully grasped this fundamental mindset of the Bordeau family, because I'd never experienced anything like it up close and personal (with exceptions of my years observing Stuart's unsuccessful pursuit of it and Jon Prioleau's pretense of having it already). Now I understood better Raven and Constantia's ramped-up interest in consumer goods after spending time with Daddy and Giselle, or Daddy and Mommy Giselle as the modern stepmother was teaching them to call her. My adversaries had been more formidable than I'd first thought. By the time I woke up to their hidden motive, their desire to take Raven and Constantia away from me permanently and exclusively, they had already won every key battle of the war. And though I somehow managed to turn the tide at the last moment, the cost of victory, if one could call the current mess a victory, had been deadly.

Raven, Constantia, and I were victims of an evil campaign. So why, now that it had been dismantled, were my insides still tied in knots? I had done what was necessary to unravel it. Why then did I feel the need to explain my actions and be vindicated by law enforcement or anyone else? Why couldn't I take Rennie's advice, cut my losses, and move forward with what I had salvaged?

Rennie laid out her take on the matter with no subtlety. "What are you, Arly...a moron? Protecting Raven and Constantia is more important than taking a chance on going to jail. And for what? To rid yourself of useless guilt?"

Nevertheless, I wanted to know the why of everything that had happened. And, God help me, I still do.

35

I survived the post memorial service reception by holding onto Raven and Constantia's warm hands. Rennie ran interference at every turn. Whenever anyone got too near, she would jump in with inane small talk, although she did not have to resort to this much. The few attendees looked to be in the age range of Stuart and Giselle's parents. And as most people, they were interested in others like themselves, not those decades younger.

Later, back in the hotel room, Rennie commented on the fact that Stuart and Giselle seemed to have no friends or acquaintances their own age. This was easy to explain considering neither of them participated in the world of work, which meant they had no built-in colleagues obligated to show up and pay respects at their double memorial service. And they traveled too much to become known entities in any one local community. According to Rennie, self-proclaimed roll keeper at the service, the one youngish person in attendance other than ourselves, was the woman who'd made it a point to tell us how much she had enjoyed having Raven and

Constantia in her four-year-old kindergarten class. She was a pretty lady, the kind of fresh-faced teacher I longed to be. I liked her the moment I met her. It warmed my heart Raven and Constantia had been in her partial care, though their being enrolled in any preschool in Florida was more damning evidence of Stuart and Giselle's treachery.

Rennie took care to speak to everyone at the gathering. She made a special point of going to the grief-stricken parents of both Stuart and Giselle, clasping their hands in hers in turn, offering them heartfelt sympathy, and lingering with each couple a full minute to add credence to her sincerity. I found it odd how grateful they were for this attention. Never mind they had no idea who Rennie was or why she was there.

The affair went smoothly enough, though the four grieving hosts were in a worse fog than I. And yet, Giselle's mother managed to summon the strength to say one disturbing thing that stood out. She stared up at me from the chair some kind soul had brought her in which to collapse. Then she said with a jagged edge, "I hope you're satisfied now. You won't have to share the children with us ever again."

Her words sent a chill up my spine. I tried to suppress it, but it grew colder. "That was bad," Rennie whispered as she guided the twins and me away from the despondent hostess. "She could be trouble."

I wished Rennie had not sounded so fearful. I wanted to believe no guile was in the old woman's statement, that all she was trying to do was express how much she had enjoyed playing the role of grandma for a little while, and her words had just come out wrong.

But Rennie believed no such thing. Which disturbed me because I knew she could be on to something. What if Giselle's mother had already seen through me? What if she set about convincing everyone around her that I had something sinister to do with Giselle's death? What if she and her husband became fixated on the idea and began working against me? What if they would not stop until they succeeded in having me arrested?

At the first signs the reception was breaking up, Rennie shepherded her three charges – Raven, Constantia, and me – toward the doorway to the hall and out into the unseasonable heat. We were walking toward the rental car with the children at a slow pace when for the first time since the shooting, I picked up on something that Rennie missed. I lifted my eyes from the sidewalk and spied a slim, mustachioed man across the street, leaning against a car, smoking a cigarette, minding his own business...not. Under normal circumstances, I would have known he was Detective Smythe even at a distance. But after enduring the pressures associated with the harrowing memorial service and reception, it took me a little longer to be sure. It was Smythe all right. No one but. He nodded in my direction. I wasn't affected by his presence at first, not made more nervous or paranoid than I already was. I think keenly irritated would be the right phrase to describe my feelings on spying him, no matter that he was staring at me with revulsion in his eyes, as if I were a murd...I meant to say common criminal? Is that you, Eve? You look as if you have something to hide. Who's that with you...the serpent?

I looked Smythe straight in the face without acknowledging his nod. He took another pull on his cigarette and stared back, unblinking, the most finely-tuned skill in his arsenal. Oh, it's you, he seemed to be thinking, feigning. What a coincidence, our meeting up like this.

Rennie did not spot him right away. Raven and Constantia's advanced case of crankiness was dominating her attention. "Look," I whispered to the perfect devastation of her already bad day. "It's Smythe."

"What? Who?"

"Smythe..." I said again, "...across the street."

She halted, adjusted her gaze, inhaled abruptly. She would have cursed but for the tender ears of the twins. Was that a malicious smile playing around the stalker's mustache? He waved to us. Rennie dropped Raven's hand and waved back. I waved to no one. Why encourage bad mojo?

Rennie regained her composure in a breath. She placed Raven and Constantia's hands in mine and told the three of us to stay put. I watched as she strode across the street, dodging traffic, looking too confident to be believable, and confronted the detective.

As Rennie approached, Smythe retreated back into his bored act, dropped his cigarette to the pavement, ground it out with his shoe sole, straightened his arthritic spine as best he could, and waited for whatever challenge Reynolds Brentwood intended to present. I was thankful to have slipped into second place on his radar. Rennie walked right up to him and stuck out her hand. He shook it. They chatted. From where I was standing across the street, their encounter appeared to be low-key. Though I knew better than to relax. In fact, I tensed up more when Smythe gestured toward me with his Florida-tanned forefinger. Rennie shook her head no. He gestured again. This time she responded by turning on her heel and traversing the street again.

As she got nearer to the girls and me, I noticed her coloring was different, somewhere between ash-gray and pea-green. I wished the pavement would open up and swallow every one of us. "Get in the car," she said. "We have to get out of here before I have a nervous breakdown. He thinks you know something. I'm sure of it."

"What could I know?" I said in a pant. "And why did he come here of all places?"

Rennie gave me a disdainful look, then she took over Raven and Constantia again and hustled them toward the car and into the backseat, this time taking pains with their booster seats loaned to us by the rental car company. I followed her and did not complain when she shoved me into the front passenger side. "I'm scared, Rennie. What do you think he's after?"

"He's after you," she said and shut the car door on the hem of my funeral dress.

And there you have it, I thought, observing the crushed silk caught within the door's greasy hinge. Trapped in every possible way.

36

On returning to the hotel, Rennie began the task of packing our belongings to the nerve-wracking background noise of Raven and Constantia badgering their mother. There was no end to the places the two scamps could think up as destinations: the pool, snack bar, jungle-gym lot, arcade room, anywhere but the stuffy connecting bedroom we had been calling theirs. In self-defense, I ignored them and began badgering Rennie, who began badgering Hal.

"Will you get these two whine-boxes out of here," she said to him through clamped teeth. "They're getting on my last nerve."

Helpful Hal whistled to Raven and Constantia like the Pied Piper and had them laughing before they made it to the hallway. "I hear there's a secret play area you haven't seen yet," he said, "with swings and seesaws for big girls. Or do you want to go back to the baby lot?"

"Big girl lot, big girl lot," shouted the little girls.

I restrained myself from interfering. Was this charmer now leading my children to fun-land the same villain who had helped

Stuart and Giselle with their loathsome plan? Why was it Raven and Constantia were always so blasted happy in the clutches of people who cared nothing about them, indeed, who may hurt them? I felt like spanking their bottoms.

"Silence is golden," Rennie said. "If it hadn't been for Hal, I'd have gone to the slammer days ago for child abuse, sent there, no doubt by that sneaky Smythe."

"I don't like it when he's alone with Raven and Constantia," I said.

"Smythe? Huh?"

"Not him…Hal"

Rennie sniggered with bitterness. "Hal ain't the enemy, darling. Those other people are."

"What other people?" I said with stupid sincerity, brain fog having crept back in.

Rennie lifted a brow and batted her eyelashes. "You cannot be serious. Smythe for one; Giselle's mother for two; the entire Winter Park Police Force, for three. Hal is a ministering angel next to them."

"Why do you think he showed up again, the Smythe guy?" I said, still sincere, still dense as mud.

Rennie looked me up and down to determine whether I had lost the rest of my mind. "Uhhh…" she said. "Could it be he's nosing around for information?" Her sarcasm fell flat, my brain being too fried to catch it.

I nodded thoughtfully. She nodded back thoughtfully, mimicking my stupefied behavior, then she went back to stuffing lingerie into her gym bag. "He said he just popped by to tell us he was having trouble sleeping. Can't get Stuart's note off his mind. What a colossal windbag, trying to throw me off with his bogus cop act."

Rennie's words frightened me. I walked over and put the chain up on the hotel room door. She sniffed at the futility of such a ridiculous precaution and sped up her efforts at packing with no help from me. "Listen, girlfriend," she said. "Your job is to stay cool no matter what. I don't mind telling you I'm worried you won't. Sheesh, you don't act like you know where you are most of the time, much less what would happen if you started running off at the mouth. It's like you're trying as hard as you can to take Hal and me down with you."

I squeezed my eyes shut to collect myself. No, I did not want to take Hal and Rennie down with me. I wanted the nightmare never to have happened. Opening my tired eyes, I glanced around the room for something to do. Yes, packing. That would be useful. I went over to the bed and tried to unzip my gym bag, but no matter how hard I tugged, the zipper refused to budge. I sank to my knees before the bed and began weeping again. Rennie paused in her own frantic packing efforts and knelt beside me. She wrapped her arms around my shoulders and comforted me one more patient time.

"I'm sorry, sweetie," she said. "I keep forgetting what you've been through. Stuart and Giselle…Raven and Constantia… Smythe. Just remember...Hal and I are doing our best to get you out of this nightmare. Don't cry anymore. We're all in it together, the three of us, a team."

37

Our flight from Orlando to Charleston was late on departure and late on arrival, the reason we slept past nine, if fitfully, in the cottage the next morning. Last to awaken, I panicked when I realized what time it was, fearful Raven and Constantia had not had their breakfast.

"Rennie," I called out on my way through the living room to the kitchen. "Is anyone here?"

Rennie came moping out of her and Hal's bedroom. Like me, she was still in her bathrobe. "Hey," she said. "Did you sleep okay? I was worried."

"Where are the girls? Have they had some cereal or fruit or anything?"

"Ice cream at seven thirty. But don't be mad. Hal packed them up a little while ago and took them over to Mama Chloe's for bacon and eggs."

"Ice cream?" I was gearing up to deliver the same junk-food lecture I used to deliver to two other people. Should I have gone ahead and said to Rennie, "Do you not remember what happened to the last two characters who fed my children junk food?" Mercifully, lock noises at the kitchen door interrupted my insane thoughts.

"Raven? Constantia?" I shouted.

"It's me," Hal said. He peeped around the corner into the living room where Rennie and I were still winding each other up. He stared at us in our robes and slippers. We stared back at him in his jeans and tie-dyed tee.

"You're awake," he said in my direction a wee bit too upbeat for my Bengal tigress mood. "Hope you're feeling better."

"I'm not...didn't sleep well. Where are Raven and Connie?"

Mrs. Lupio saw us when we drove up. Asked if they could come over for milk and cookies. I didn't think you'd mind. They had a good breakfast."

"Milk," Rennie chimed in. "We don't have that, either. Somebody needs to take their whole paycheck and give it up to that over-priced organic food store in Mount Pleasant. Cupboard is as bare as Lady Godiva's butt."

I turned on her with a vengeance. "I wish you'd tell the truth for once, Rennie. Breakfast sandwiches are in the freezer, granola bars in the pantry, and oatmeal in a cannister..."

"Truth?" said Rennie. She walked to the couch and let herself down slowly as if suffering from the worst effects of a hangover. Then she spoke again in a grumble, one she wanted me to hear. "I know you didn't just use the word truth with a straight face."

Hal ducked back into the kitchen to escape what appeared to be the beginning of a catfight.

"Yes," I said. "Truth. It's what I plan to tell the authorities and everyone else in Florida as soon as I get my wits about me."

Rennie wrapped her robe tighter across her triple-D chest. "Don't talk to me about truth. Do you honestly think Giselle's mother wants to hear truth? That you killed her daughter on account of you found out, for certain, she was trying to take your children? I had an abortion when I was sixteen. Do you think my mother wants to know that in the name of truth? And Hal...he's been involved with a married woman a couple of months now... me. Do you think a conservative Texan like my husband, Clark, wants to hear any of the disgusting details if Hal and I got ideas about clearing our consciences? No, he doesn't, and you're not going to salve your conscience by telling Giselle's mother the gory facts about her daughter's death. In this situation, your brand of truth doesn't match up with what is right. I'm appalled by your selfishness."

"Yeah, well, you aren't the one who did the shooting. It's driving me out of my mind. I can't live with it."

Rennie placed her right palm flat against her forehead. "My head feels like it's caught in a vice," she said. "This must be the point where people involved in a crime start getting suspicious of each other. It's only been the last couple of hours I grasped the risk Hal and I took for you. And now I'm wondering if it was worth it. Or if I'm going to come back to the cottage one day and find you singing like a canary to some officer of the law. Isn't it enough I have to sweat Smythe figuring everything out all by his lonesome? No, it isn't. I have to worry about you getting on the phone with him and spilling your guts. Which would cook my and Hal's goose to the bone. And Raven and Contantia's too. They could kiss their mother goodbye, same as their father. And then they'd have to do a quick little turn-around and say hello to Giselle and Stuart's parents, their new caregivers. Did you notice how old those people are? Your thinking is way off, Arlena, and I'm sick to death of it. I want you to tell me once and for all, how do you intend to play this out?"

"I already said…I'm going to talk to an official the minute I'm able, someone who knows the law, who can tell me the best way to go about owning up to what I did without hurting you or Hal or the girls. But I promise not to do anything that can't be undone, not until I get to the bottom of what to expect."

"And how do you plan to find this hypothetical, mythical, unbiased, trustworthy expert on the law to answer your hypothetical, mythical, dumb questions?"

"Somebody still in law school, maybe. Or a criminal attorney here in town. I'd hate to put Mr. Pinckney in the hot seat again, although he is trustworthy. What do you think? Would it be better to talk to a professional not biased in my favor? I don't know if Mr. Pinckney is still up on codes. He hasn't practiced law for years."

Hal hadn't said a word during this loud exchange. He had gotten busy in the kitchen washing ice cream bowls, wiping down counters, cleaning the inside of the microwave, mopping the floor. It's what he did when he got nervous. He cleaned. The cottage was spotless of late.

Rennie called to him from the sofa. "Get in here, Hal. Talk some sense into her."

He peered around the corner from the kitchen again, this time his gaze focused on Rennie, who said to him in complete dejection, "Man…Hal…it's so worse than I thought. Do you want to give it a try?"

Hal answered her with his eyes. No, he did not want to give it a try. A good thing. Why would Rennie think I'd ever listen to an opinion of Hal's in all our shared lifetimes? I watched as he slipped into the sitting room and leaned against a wall, his lanky build in stark contrast to Rennie's voluptuous curves. From the beginning they had formed an alliance against me, one growing stronger by the second. They had taken over my home, my time, my life, and now my problems and future.

"Look, Rennie," I said, though I was also addressing Hal. "I appreciate everything you've done for me, both of you."

Rennie squinched her face. "No, stop. You don't appreciate a thing. Here's the way it's going to be from now on. We all have a big fat secret, and we're all going to keep it, the three of us, including you, Arlena. For crying out loud, you're the one who caused the problem."

"I never asked you and Hal to drive to Florida."

"Oh-h-h," Rennie said. "You make me so mad, I feel like choking you. Hal, do you remember what we talked about yesterday? Are you ready?"

Rennie's clearly reluctant assistant tensed and stepped away from the wall. "Yes," he said, his voice soft. He moved closer to Rennie. I shuffled backward as Rennie rose from the sofa and positioned herself next to Hal. They were both facing me now, as coiled and calm as Detective Smythe.

"Arlena," Rennie said with uncharacteristic seriousness. "We're no longer asking you to use good judgment. We're telling you. If you refuse, we're going to take steps."

The normally carefree Rennie had never spoken to me in such a tone. No way was I letting her get away with it. "Are you threatening me?" I said. "What do you mean take steps?"

"I mean...whatever."

I wheeled around and began pacing. I was so angry at Rennie I could have...could have what? Shot her? Why didn't she see the truth had to be told? Why did she think lying was better?

"He has already done enough to me," I said to Rennie, referring to and pointing toward Hal. "And you aren't going to add to it. The entire problem could have been avoided if Junior-G-Man there had told me what Stuart and Giselle were up to. But no...he went along with them for money. Using them, me, and you, too, Rennie. You're nothing to him but the current older woman. Who do you think you are...Mrs. Robinson? And what about Clark? Somehow I don't see a Texas oil baron thinking this was all my fault. Because it wasn't. It was your fault too, for letting Hal move in on top of us. And Hal's for taking money from Stuart to spy on me. And not just spy on me, lie through his teeth about me. The two of you make me want to puke."

I stumbled around the living room in my fury, kicking at furniture, yelling, venting emotions I did not know I still had. Right then I was angrier at Rennie than at Hal. For all I cared at that volcanic moment, Smythe could arrest them both and initiate a dual trial.

Rennie's face went from maroon to ash as my tantrum melted away. She said nothing. I slunk to the sofa and flopped down. No more raging around the living room. No more making speeches. Just sinking into deeper despair. I wanted to cry again, but could not. Hopeless thoughts flooded my brain. Thoughts of Raven, Constantia, Rennie, Hal, and me, five lost souls teetering on the edge of a chasm. What were the chances of any of us surviving? "Help me," I cried out to no one. "What am I going to do? I can't go on like this."

For once, Rennie stayed silent. I lifted my gaze to her face in expectation of a sympathetic response. Why wasn't she flying across the room to comfort me...to hold me in the same caring way she'd been doing since Florida? My tirade had left exhaustion in its wake. I craved comfort. I needed Rennie to sit with me while

I cried myself to sleep again. I couldn't fathom why she was just standing there rooted in the same spot next to Hal. I felt remorseful and miserable about lambasting her and was about to say how sorry I was, but then my nose began to leak, the small interruption of which made me forget my good intentions.

I was weak and out of control, but Hal and Rennie were neither. I saw when he glanced at Rennie with resolve in his eyes, and I wondered why she nodded back. My gaze flitted back and forth between the two of them. What was going on here? What was this new purpose glittering in their eyes?

Alarmed, I leapt from the sofa and raced for the kitchen. I had decided. I was calling the police. But Hal stopped me as I grabbed for the wall phone. He held me tightly from behind, pinning my arms to my sides. As I struggled and kicked, he lifted me off the floor and carried me to the sofa in the living room, where, maintaining a sure grip, he got me situated in a seated position next to him.

Then Rennie, with great difficulty due to my thrashing legs, stuffed a cloth into my mouth. Hal held my arms fast as she pressed a strip of tape across the cloth to muffle my cries. I flailed against her with my legs and feet, but Hal maintained his grip, against which, being weak, I made no progress.

Then Rennie stepped to the side out of my reach. I gave up kicking and followed her with my eyes. Her expression was no longer stone. She was the one crying now, stricken of face, stooped of body. I did not know what else to do except continue my struggle with Hal, though my strength was quickly dissipating. Within seconds, I gave in to sobbing, my back against his chest. He loosened his grip so that I could breathe easier. Then he began crooning to me. "It's all right, Arlena," he said. "Everything is going to be all right. Rest now…rest."

On hearing those insulting words, I strained my muscles one last time before weakness overcame me again. Hal was wrong. Things were never going to be all right again. Unable to fight any longer, I dropped my head and wept.

Rennie stepped close again and knelt in front of me face-to-face. "Arlena, love…Hal doesn't want to hurt you. He isn't going to hurt you. But you've come unhinged. We think you might be having a nervous breakdown. You could end up in a hospital somewhere if you can't find a resting place for your mind. Will you stop resisting now? I have some medicine I can give you, but I won't if you'll settle down. Let us help you, Arly…please. Can you walk to the bed without Hal having to carry you?"

On hearing Rennie's distressing phrases – find a resting place for your mind, end up in a hospital, doesn't want to hurt you, stop resisting – I used up my last ounce of strength to let her know I was going nowhere with her or Hal…not willingly. And when she reached out a hand to try to calm me, she found out I meant it. It was then I saw the "medicine." Hal turned my body to the side by force and held me still so that Rennie could jab my arm with a needle. I went on struggling like the mental case I had become…until the drug took effect…after which I slipped into unconsciousness. As I faded, I heard Hal whisper something strange into my ear. Even today I wonder why he said it at such a desperate moment. "I love you, Arlena. I'm so sorry for everything. I honestly love you."

And then everything went black.

38

Rennie's assessment of my condition proved correct. I did need to find a resting place for my mind. And after she administered the merciful medication via the unmerciful needle (last in the latest series of unfortunate events that escaped my memory for days), I floated to a land of peaceful repose and healing where I remained for much of the weekend.

It was incredible how much calmer I felt on waking. The second I opened my eyes, I realized I had made a change. Turning over to stretch, I bumped into the snoozing Rennie. I smiled at her Mickey Mouse pajamas and funny sleep-face...mouth a'gape, drool a'drip. "Hey, you," I said. "Wake up. You're snoring like a moose."

Whereupon my friend scrambled to her knees, wide-eyed, tousled, stinky of breath. She began babbling, gesticulating, praying aloud. "Dear God. Thank you, God. Thank you, thank you. Oh, Arlena, I thought I'd killed you. But you're okay. I mean, you're good, right?"

"Thirsty…and I need to go to the bathroom."

Rennie laughed aloud as I yawned my way through a short pause. "What time is it? Are the girls still asleep?"

My friend gave me a confused look before answering. I was unable to read the question in her eyes. Though it must not have been important. She blocked it forthwith. "Oh…the girls," she said. "They're probably on the beach with Hal."

Another pause. Another satisfying yawn on my part. Another strange question from Rennie, this time verbal. "You aren't mad at me?" she said. "About…you know?"

It was my turn to look confused. "Should I be? What have you done?"

"Uh…nothing. Not a thing. Let's just say for once in the history of mankind, certain skills required for the enjoyment of recreational drugs saved the total day."

"What are you talking about?"

"Forget it. Go to the bathroom. I'll get some hot tea going."

"What time is it?"

Rennie glanced at the slim Cartier on her plump wrist. "Six thirty."

"Pretty early, huh, for Raven and Constantia to be playing on the beach."

It's six thirty at night, darling, not morning."

⌘ ⌘ ⌘

Later in the afternoon, Rennie and I sat together in the sunroom, munching on cheese toast and savoring English tea. Every minute or so I marveled aloud about how something as simple as restful sleep could help a person.

Rennie set down her mug and blew her nose into a paper napkin. "Glad somebody's been helped. I personally have a splitting headache, an upset stomach, and a fever."

"Oh, no. I'm sorry, Ren. You need rest too." I didn't tell Rennie the word rest had triggered a troubling something in my brain, though I could not put my finger on what.

Rennie dragged her hands down her face and then laced her fingers in her lap where she stared at them as if she had never seen them before. For a second I thought she might break into a yoga ohmmmm. But she did not. She gave herself thirty seconds of prep time before bringing her gaze, now fully alert, back to my surprised face. "We have to talk" she said. "But not tonight. Tonight, we have to get the girls fed and bathed, pampered and storied, and early to bed. Hal's on his last leg worse than I am. Mrs. Lupio said she'd watch the girls a few hours in the morning. We can talk then."

"You're worrying too much, Ren. We don't need to talk. Everything is going to be fine, now that I've decided…"

"Stop with your I've decided." Rennie clenched her teeth in an unattractive manner. She was in bad shape physically and emotionally. Puffy, bluish bags drooped beneath her blood-shot eyes. For the first time in our lives, Rennie looked old to me. I wondered if I looked old to her.

"But I have, Ren…decided. And I feel so much better for it."

Rennie rubbed her tired eyes before responding. "Is that supposed to make me feel better?" she said. "'Cause it doesn't. It makes me feel worse."

⌘ ⌘ ⌘

Next morning, Rennie and I sat at the kitchen bar sipping second mugs of strong coffee. Hal was quiet as usual as he cleared away the breakfast things and puttered back and forth between the fridge and sink. Raven and Constantia had taken their noisiness over to Mrs. Lupio's. Rennie, unfortunately, had not.

"Face it," she said to me after another obnoxious slurp of Starbucks. "Giselle's mother and father will try to discredit you the first opportunity they get. Stuart's parents, too. They want Raven and Constantia for themselves…no different from Stuart and Giselle in that respect."

My muscles constricted at Rennie's plain insight. Why did it always and forevermore come back around to someone trying to take my children? I resented Ren for destroying my new-found serenity (acquired from the peaceful rest afforded me by the syringe full of medicine administered by her, with Hal's help, the memory of which still lay hidden deep within my subconscious).

I stared into my empty mug and sulked, an unhelpful reaction that was wasted on the hyper Rennie. All morning she had been racing along on her own private zip-line greased with frayed nerves and too much caffeine, hearing and seeing things that may or may not have been there: a police car cruising by the cottage; Detective Smythe walking on the beach clad in tan trench coat and fedora; a van with the call numbers of a local TV news show stenciled on its side pulling into a neighbor's driveway. I had to work at resisting panic myself as I watched her pace back and forth, muttering to herself, asking unanswerable questions. Were we being watched? Were the authorities withholding information? Had they collected enough evidence to bring us in if we made one more stupid mistake?

By this time, I do believe my own head remained the coolest in our company, an unsettling circumstance given the absurdity of my thinking. So far, I'd been more of a hindrance than a help. It was Rennie who had managed to hold things together. But now she was the one unraveling, fretting, gnawing at her acrylic nails. And Hal, well, I thought for sure he would scrub the finish right off the stainless-steel sink. I felt sorry for both of them and wished they could find the same peace I had found. Fiddle on, Nero. Burn, baby, burn. It was so lovely abiding in the delusion that my confession would solve all our problems.

I would have already let every cat out of the bag if Rennie had not kept hammering me with reality. Not even personal exhaustion deterred her. Against growing odds, she kept shoving the obvious down my throat - the fact that easing my own conscience was not worth losing my children. "What's the matter with you?" she'd say. "Why can't you see confessing is the worst possible thing you could do? You have to stay quiet, protect your future, bring your children up in a normal environment."

And then she would drill me again about how much she and Hal had risked to keep me out of prison, how they'd sacrificed everything for me, how I owed them my undying loyalty and cooperation, and how she could not believe my ingratitude. I admit now I'm glad she did not get tired of repeating herself, particularly when it came to the recurring finale with which she closed every speech: If you love Raven and Constantia, you'll stop your kamikaze act. Do you love them? Will you stop self-destructing?"

"Of course," I would say then. "I love my children more than anything in the world, and, yes, I do want to stop self-destructing."

The problem was I did not have a firm idea of what that would look like in real terms. It was a good beginning to want to, though, which was the reason I agreed, if under duress, not to make an immediate phone call. This was a huge concession considering the weight of remorse in my heart. It slashed at me at regular intervals, inflaming my emotions, disrupting my ability to think straight. When my distress would became unbearable, I'd forget my gratefulness to Rennie and Hal, my responsibility to Raven and Constantia, even my own future. I would give in again to my need for personal punishment to put things right...find myself literally yearning for it.

But Rennie was having none of this self-absorbed nuttiness as she so touchingly referred to my questionable desires. Her intention was to stomp out every spark of false virtue. Though exhausted herself, she still made sure she was always there to talk me through my steady flow of warped reasoning. And I listened, unconvinced more often than not as she articulated her slippery suppositions, the most creative of which was that Stuart and Giselle had been responsible for their own demise. Rennie had never liked Stuart, not from the first, and definitely not after I married him. She called him an arrogant, pseudo, intellectual snob with champagne taste and a beer wallet. She said he was way worse than the guy I had married straight out of high school. "That wasn't even a marriage," she would declare every time I brought it up. "It was more like a boyfriend/girlfriend thing…going steady for a while." She worked hard at convincing me with her slippery arguments. "Stuart is the only real husband you've ever had to put up with. And he just wanted you around to shine up his credibility, not 'cause he loved you. You were his arm candy. But the worst was that he worked you like a farm animal to feed his own greediness."

I thought Rennie had it backward, that I was the user. To me, Stuart tipped any scale to the positive on smooth, smart, and handsome. I never understood what he saw in me, the consummate nerd. Having a cool guy like Stuart in my life seemed an amazing gift to enjoy rather than analyze. Until I discovered the "cool gift" had so little substance. But even after the damage I suffered at his hands, I still found it difficult to hear Rennie describe in painstaking detail the many heartaches Stuart had inflicted on me from the beginning. And even harder to hear her chronicle Giselle's sins, of which bad taste and selfishness were the least and trying to steal my children the worst. Bottom line? Rennie believed Stuart and Giselle had gotten precisely what they deserved, and I was simply the instrument used by the universe to level cosmic justice.

At times her slick arguments made a weird form of sense. "What goes around comes around," she'd say when she could think of nothing else. It was a quote approaching accuracy, but not bull's eye. Even so, I sank deeper into misery every time she said it. Could it be true? Could the entire repugnant affair be boiled down to a single, tired cliché? What goes around, comes around? How stinking pathetic.

Every time I attempted to describe my feelings of hopelessness to Rennie, she would turn them around on me with the oddest supposition of all, that I, Arlena, had made the supreme sacrifice of committing a crime punishable by death just to save my children. It was a stretch more fantasy than exaggeration. Even in my compromised state of mind, I was able to recognize its dishonesty. I knew I had initiated the Florida fiasco to protect myself as much as Raven and Constantia. It was my intention to tear them out of the clutches of Stuart and Giselle for my own selfish needs. How then could this be the supreme sacrifice? In those critical hours before the shooting, hadn't the children become possessions so precious that the avaricious adults in their lives, including me, would commit any grievous sin to have them, keep them, possess them?

Rennie agreed the twins were possessions in the eyes of Stuart and Giselle. "But not in yours, Arlena. They are your flesh and blood. You can't equate ownership of a diamond ring with ownership of one's heart. Vital organs aren't possessions. They're the stuff of life. And make no mistake, Raven and Constantia are that and more. When you shot Giselle, you were fighting for your children. Maybe you fought in the wrong way, could have resolved things differently. Though I don't see how. Stuart and Giselle were relentless, ruthless. Their intention was to cut you out of the twins' lives permanently."

"But I didn't have to kill her. Hal had already stopped feeding Stuart information by the time I found out what was going on. I could tell by the dates in his journal. I allowed myself to go insane because I wanted to go insane. I felt entitled, justified."

"Hindsight is twenty-twenty. You had no way of knowing what Hal would have done ultimately. Oh, he's sorry now all right. But back then? I don't think he knows, either, not for sure. You had nothing to go on except what you found in the trunk, hard evidence of him helping Stuart and Giselle stab you in the back. How else could you have defended yourself. It was a certainty Stuart and Giselle had no intention of letting Raven and Constantia come back home. They were prepared to put you through years of suffering in court. I've done a lot of thinking about this, and I can't come up with any other effective means of defending yourself but what you did. Nothing short of violence was going to work. You had no choice."

"Rennie, tell me you know I did not set out to hurt Giselle on purpose. It was like…someone else pulled the trigger. That's all I want to tell the police. It was an accident. I swear to you, I didn't mean to hurt her."

"I believe you, same as I believe Hal. Who knows? Maybe, you didn't do it by yourself. Maybe, some supernatural force got in control. I don't know about things like that. But I do know those two jerks in Florida were after Raven and Constantia, and you risked everything to stop them. You're still at risk. Your mind is messed up from shock…temporarily, I hope. Hal and I are sticking close by until you get through this. Cripes, I've never done much thinking in my whole life, not about anything, and here I am having to think for all three of us in a monster situation. Feels like a bomb is ticking inside my head. Please, please…hang tough a little longer, Arly. And I will, too, and Hal. I promise, we won't let you down."

39

I told Rennie I wasn't together enough to go back to school, that the children at Wellington would run me out of the building if they did not have my full attention. No weakling should ever walk into an elementary classroom, student teaching obligation or no. But Rennie would not hear of my calling in sick another day. According to her, I had been home from Florida long enough for any ex-wife to deal with a tragedy in the immediate family of an ex-husband. Raven and Constantia were back in playschool; Rennie and Hal in their own classes; and I had only a few days left to finish my student teaching requirement, the final stamp of approval required for certification in South Carolina. I would reach my goal of being officially qualified to teach in a public school where Raven and Constantia could attend as students.

It was smart of Rennie to lean on the argument that I had no choice. Apparently, she believed this a true axiom concerning all matters of importance in my life. I knew for certain her instincts were good, not bad, and she was putting the children's welfare first, not her own, nor Hal's, nor mine. But I wasn't sure I could muster the strength to face Wellington. And yet it was also true I could not allow Stuart and Giselle take away my ability to make a living for my children in addition to everything else. I had already lost enough to them – peace of mind, self-respect, time with Raven and Constantia, the comfort of being an ordinary citizen with no past. And I needed a path to a secure job. I viewed Miss Peregrine's generosity as a bridge to independence, not dependence. I wanted to stand on my own two feet for the sake of my children.

Rennie repeated my responsibility to me over and over: You owe it to Raven and Constantia to finish your academic requirements and support them as a good mother, whether you feel able or not. And she punctuated each reminder by stating the possibility that if I languished in depression too long after returning home from Florida, it might suggest I had something to hide. She said my and Raven and Constantia's lives should go forward with our regular routines. For the girls, this meant no more missed days at playschool. For me, no incompletes for credit hours, no falling apart in the classroom, and no emotional outbursts or drawing attention to myself. My own life, in particular, had to proceed in a manner revealing every transparent detail. I could not afford to raise suspicion in the eyes of a certain respected law enforcement official in Florida, the shrewd Detective Smythe.

Thus, the next morning, again under duress, I showered and dressed in my plainest black slacks and white blouse and spent twenty minutes organizing my school bag. Hal and Rennie did their part by feeding the girls and getting them ready for playschool. I forced myself to keep slogging through my morning home routine despite the series of horrifying flashbacks flitting across my mind: rain beating on glass doors; Stuart inching toward me with malice in his eyes; a single gunshot; blood; Giselle lying dead in her own living room sprawled across her expensive Mediterranean tile and priceless Oriental rug; Stuart dropping down beside her, lifting her upper body to his own heaving chest, embracing and rocking her, crying over her, urging her to wake up.

I would be in the process of something as simple as buttoning my blouse, and for no reason find myself staring into space; or put one shoe on and forget the other; or brush my hair in front and leave it ratty in back; or fasten my wristwatch on upside down; or go into the bathroom to brush my teeth and end up cleaning the toilet.

Rennie and Hal made it their business to redirect my mental misfires. Every time they caught me in a downward slide, they snatched me back to the present, no discussion, no mercy. At this point, Rennie didn't trust me on my own for anything. And she was smart not to. I heard her tell Hal that her hope was I had been at Wellington long enough, five weeks, to know my class down to the last detail and could get through the last few days on automatic pilot. However, my hope was not in myself, but in my students. Their energy and love could transcend anything.

I don't know if Hal had a hope. If he did, he chose not to share it. He simply went along obeying Rennie's commands with the faithfulness of an old dog. And yet the expression on his narrow face, far more thin and fox-like now than in the days before Florida, remained fixed in an uncomfortable mask. He watched after me like a bodyguard, anticipated my every need, jumped to do things I was able to do for myself. I paid his compulsive behavior no attention at first, my shock being too profound to notice. But after a while, it became annoying. I couldn't reach for a glass before he jumped to get it for me. Or sit on the sofa without his rushing to put a pillow at my back. I couldn't do anything without him getting in my way. But then, without knowing how or why, I found myself expecting his help. I liked for him to carry my school bag to the car, chauffeur me, hang back in corners and doorways like a guardian angel in case I might need any little thing. Rennie concerned herself with my future; Hal took care of my daily needs. Running a hot bath for a person who has been beaten down by the world is kindness. Putting clean towels by the tub, lighting candles that smell of lavender, and placing a steaming mug of tea on the bedside table…these considerations of Hal's exceeded kindness and moved into the realm of love.

40

I made it through my first day back at school with few bumps. When Hal picked me up after the last bell, he was overjoyed to hear of my success. His face became the picture of relief. And though I wanted to hang onto my animosity toward him, it was good to see him smile.

He and I were peculiar traveling companions on our way back to Sullivan's Island, neither of us talking. It was not long before the silence lulled me to sleep in the passenger seat of the Explorer. The day had been exhausting, and after I found out from Hal that Raven and Constantia were playground-hopping in Mount Pleasant with their Aunt Rennie, I relaxed and gave in to a much-needed nap.

From which I did not awaken until Hal made a strange sound in his throat on pulling into the cottage driveway. I rubbed my eyes to force myself alert. "Hal?" I said. "Are you getting a cold?"

"I wish that were it. Look who's waiting for us."

I could not believe what I was saw…Detective Smythe was seated on the bottom back step, forearms resting on knees, lit cigarette adding to the stains on his fingers. My eyes shifted back and forth between the cigarette and the Florida license plate on his vehicle. "Do you think he's here…to arrest me?" I said.

"Stay calm. You've done everything right…school, home, everything."

"You don't sound calm. You sound like you're about to jump out of your skin."

Hal's breath came in shallow puffs when he breathed at all. "What if we just drove away?" he said, and then, "Oh, no. He's standing up. It would look weird to cut and run now."

Hal opened the Explorer door and made slow moves to get out. I remained in the passenger seat, squinting at the object of my attention on the steps. "Did he just flick his cigarette butt onto my driveway?" I said aloud to myself. "He's a bigger ass than I thought, flicking a cigarette butt on somebody else's property."

I opened the passenger door, climbed out, and closed the door with unnecessary force. Hal had to hustle to catch up with me as I hoofed it across the concrete drive toward Smythe, who now had an alarmed expression on his face. Hal grabbed my arm mid-driveway and panted out a few nonsensical phrases. "Wait a minute… wait. What are you doing?"

I looked up at him, irritated. "What I've wanted to do from the start, tell him the truth. Now let go of my arm."

"But you can't. He'll lock Rennie and me up. You can't."

"Oh, yes, I can, and I'm going to. Let go of my arm."

Somehow, Smythe beamed himself across the driveway into my and Hal's space. "Young man," he said, "if I were you, I'd let go of her arm like she asked."

Hal obeyed his elder and looked down at his own feet in submission. I submitted to no one. I stomped over to the cigarette butt still lying in evidence, picked it up between thumb and forefinger, and held it high in the air. "My driveway is not your ashtray," I shouted at the guilty detective. "Who do you think you are?"

Hal and Smythe looked at me in astonishment for different reasons, to be sure, but equally as shocked. "Well?" I said. "Do you throw these down on everybody's private property or just mine?"

The detective's lip curled into a snarl. Said he with disgust, "Do you shoot guns on everybody's private property or just places where you hate the owners?" At that, I thought Hal might sprint. He appeared to have been shot himself.

With deranged recklessness, I glared at the two men, then marched up the back steps and let myself into the kitchen. By the time I'd tossed the cigarette butt into the trash can and washed my hands, Hal and the detective had made their way into the living room. I joined them, settling into the nearest armchair without speaking. Hal appeared on the verge of passing out or dying. An ominous green ring circled his mouth. Neither he nor Smythe would sit until I gave them permission, which I did with two disrespectful hand gestures.

"Well?" I said to the detective.

"I want to talk to you," he responded. His sleepy gaze and fake boredom had returned to his craggy face.

"And I want to talk to you," I said, tone defiant. Hal's Adam's apple went up and down, accompanied by an audible gulp. I proceeded to dig my hole deeper. "But if you insult me again, I won't. I'm tired of you trying to back me into a corner. Let's get everything out in the open once and for all."

Detective Smythe slid his gaze over to Hal. "Don't you have something to do outside, son? You look like you could use some fresh air."

The greenish Hal, always eager to please, vaulted out of the chair and practically ran to the kitchen. Smythe and I heard the door to the front stairway open, rattle, and slam. The reptile detective lifted an eyebrow and smirked. I looked away, resentful of his condescension. "Mrs. Prince," he said to my profile, "are you aware I'm about to retire from police work? This is my last week on the job after forty odd years…my last week."

I did not respond. The tenor of his announcement had the quality of an introduction, as if there would be more. I waited, insolent and silent.

"I know you killed her," he said.

One uncontrollable moan came from deep within my chest. Just one. I faced him again. "I'm glad you know. I want to talk about it."

I was going to say more, but noises from the kitchen stopped me. It sounded as if a large group of rowdies had entered through the back door. I could tell from the voices that Rennie was leading the gang accompanied by the exuberant Raven and Constantia and the non-exuberant Hal. "Arlena," Rennie shouted, her voice shrill, distraught. "Where are you? What are you doing?"

Smythe and I watched as she flew into the living room followed by the giggling twins and mute Hal. "Nothing," I said. "Detective Smythe is here."

"Heaven help us all," Rennie breathed, whispering now instead of shouting. "What have you told him? Hal says you're out of your mind again."

I gave Hal a quick, disciplinary look before defending myself to Rennie. "No, my mind is clearer than it's ever been in my life." And then I spoke briefly to Raven and Constantia. "Come here, girls. I want you to meet my friend, Mr. Smythe. Can you say hello?"

Raven gave the detective a flirty glance. Constantia buried her face in my lap. Raven, as usual, was the only child brave enough to speak. "I'm glad you're Mommy's friend. She doesn't have any other friends except for Aunt Rennie and Hal, and sometimes Mrs. Lupio."

The detective smiled again, this time without a smirk. I didn't give him a chance to speak to Raven. "Hal," I said. "Do you mind taking the girls outside to run around a little while? The beach would be good. And, Rennie, will you go too? I need to talk to Detective Smythe in private."

Hal began gathering Raven and Contantia up and hustling them through the sunroom. Rennie dug in her heels. "Listen, Arly, if it's all the same to you, I'd like to stay. You haven't been yourself lately."

"I'm fine…and I've decided. Now go. Everything is going to be okay."

Rennie looked desperate. "No, no. Think what you're doing. This is no good."

"I know exactly what I'm doing, and it's very good. By the way, before you leave, I want you to know something. I remember now what you and Hal did to me with that needle. And I know you meant well, so I don't feel vengeful. You can drop that from your worry list."

Dejected isn't a strong enough descriptor for the look on Rennie's face. I don't have a descriptor in my vocabulary that suffices. She turned and dragged herself away, glancing back over her shoulder twice with imploring looks. "Go," I mouthed to her. "I've decided."

And she went, dead-woman-walking. I watched to make sure she was out of hearing before I spoke next. When certain, I said to Detective Smythe. "I'm ready to talk now."

He shook his head violently "No way. For the sake of your children, you can't say anything."

"But I have to. You'll understand."

He shook his head again. "I may, but a judge and jury may not. Shut your mouth and listen. I don't need your confession. Nor would any other detective worth his salt. Anybody could prove you guilty without half-trying, what with forensics and credit card records and all the lies you and your so-called friends have been telling to obstruct justice. The worst is you've got a viable motive. The female victim's' mother told me how upset you were over the prospect of your children being taken out of the country, not to mention the possibility of a custody battle. You know what they say about motive, Mrs. Prince. Don't mess with a mother bear's cubs, not if you don't want your arm torn off."

He closed his eyes and dropped his head. If I hadn't known for a fact he was a crusty old cop, I would have sworn he was fighting back tears. He shuddered and re-focused. "My problem is I can't get those two little girls off my mind," he said. "It's a matter of conscience, and I don't want it on mine that I took part in any misguided legal machinations that could cause them to lose their mother to prison. But I still know you did it. And I'm not the only one. I found that out when I interviewed the female victim's mother and father. You don't have to worry about those two though. Just a couple of weak old people who can't do what it takes to get you caught. So then…congratulations, Mrs. Prince. You've gotten away with murder."

Now it was my turn to shake my head violently. "But I can't live with it."

"Oh, you're going to live with it all right. For the sake of those children out there on the beach, you're going to live with it the rest of your life. I've seen this sort of thing happen before. One parent gets done in by the other and settles the score mortally, and then the legal system steps in and sends him or her to jail, or worse than jail, and the kids get left behind with nobody. But not this time. This time we're all going to live with our choices and decisions and actions – you and me both – and those two flaky friends you run with. Do you get what I'm saying, Mrs. Prince?"

It would have been satisfying to swear I did not. Satisfying, but untrue. I got what he was saying all too well.

41

Detective Smythe rose from the armchair. He looked tired, a man more than a decade past retirement age. I stood up to show him out. But before I could make a move toward the kitchen, a sad visual caught my eye. It floated in the center pane of the far-left sunroom window. Rennie, hair wet from new rain, stood peering through. When I saw more raindrops pelting her face and splashing against the window glass, I knew Raven and Constantia would come blowing back in soon with Hal.

"Please, Detective Smythe, would you mind speaking to my friend, Rennie, before you go. It'll have to be quick. The twins will be coming in out of the rain."

"I will, but it wouldn't be prudent to divulge much. Less said the better."

"I know. It's just...she' been so faithful to try to help me."

I walked smartly through the sunroom and opened the door to the deck. "Rennie, sweetheart, come in. You're getting soaked."

Rennie's eyes were like saucers when she stepped inside. "Has he gone?" she said. "What did you tell him?"

And then she saw Smythe was still there, standing quietly in the connecting space between the living room and kitchen. She almost ran me down trying to get back outside, but I stopped her. "Don't, Ren. It's all settled. Detective Smythe is leaving now."

She was like a child in my arms. Afraid. Dependent. Confused. I felt terrible about the grief I had caused her. She yielded to my strength as I led her closer to the detective, who was no longer sleepy or coiled or bored. He had a look on his face resembling compassion as he spoke a hurried word to Rennie. "Ma'am," he said and nodded once with genuine courtesy. "I'm sorry I can't recall your name, not that it's necessary. I won't be writing it on any forms. This case is closed…for keeps."

Rennie slumped against me without taking her eyes off Smythe. "Closed?" she whispered, then she hesitated. "You mean…"

He nodded. "You can count on it. I'm the senior investigating officer in charge and in possession of the proper stamp and ink pad."

And now it was Rennie's turn to fall apart. I helped her to the sofa and let her down on the cushions to blubber aloud by herself. I had other important details to check off, the first being Smythe himself. I walked back to where he was standing to accompany him to the kitchen door. Halfway there we heard the commotion of Hal and the children coming into the sunroom off the deck, laughing, bumping into furniture, squealing with delight at getting wet in the downpour. The detective waved me away to tend to my children. "I can see myself out," he said. "You go look after those little girls."

I thrust a hand toward him for a shake. He did not look inclined, but went along with the sentimentality. His palm felt rough and warm in mine…strong, competent, old. He pulled it away and shoved it back into his pocket. He cocked his head meaningfully. "I'll always know you did it," he said again and paused. "You can play at schmoozing me if you want, but don't get the idea I'm your friend. I know you did it, and the only reason I'm walking away is for the welfare of those children in there. And maybe to make a positive difference in the way the criminal justice system works.

I'm too old now to do much about that kind of thing, but I want to go out trying. Still…I know you did it, and I know you'll suffer for it the rest of your days. High-and-mighty types like you and your friends remind me of that old come-uppance warning in the Bible – If you sow the wind, you reap the whirlwind. Hosea 8:7."

I wanted to say something more, anything to defend myself. But he would not let me. He held up a wrinkly hand to shut me up, then he turned and departed, leaving me with nothing but a sad memory of his slumped shoulders and curved spine. And that, as they say, was that. Smythe went the way of the back door, and I went the way of my children in the sunroom, grateful for the prospect of never laying eyes on Smythe again.

42

At this juncture, it is important to make you understand I did not get away with a thing. True, I was never arrested, charged, tried, convicted, sentenced, or incarcerated. Not in this life anyway. In the afterlife, things may play out differently. I have asked God for forgiveness. I've also asked him to help me forgive myself. He granted my first request in an instant. No word yet on the second.

The one individual who did not forgive me and never will, I suppose, was Smythe. He made his feelings clear beyond doubt on that last day I spoke with him. I was glad Rennie did not follow suit. When I asked for her forgiveness, she said I didn't need a thing like that from a true friend. "Darling," she said, "you're looking at a girl who's just thankful she didn't get cuffed and stuffed herself."

And since Hal's forgiveness didn't apply, I did not bother with a saccharine request. Though, curiously, he asked me to forgive him time and again. Ah, what a tyrant, the guilty conscience.

Rennie never inquired as to why I changed my mind about spilling my guts to law enforcement. I'm sure she figured I had second thoughts when I saw the guillotine about to fall on my neck. Maybe one day I'll tell her the real story, that Smythe thought my telling the truth was a worse idea than she did. As for Hal, I had no interest in what he thought. Yet who knows? Maybe one day I'll tell him the real story too. Though I imagine he doesn't care about details, only that somehow he and Rennie slid by the delights of prison.

It wasn't long before I began envying my two running buddies' happiness at being free. To me, freedom felt like punishment of a strange kind, which as you know can manifest in unexpected forms. I still wish Detective Smythe had found it in his heart to tell me he understood why I shot Giselle, not just that he knew. And I wish he had not looked at me with such contempt as he walked out of my life. I still have not deciphered the reason I wanted to run after him, crying and begging...Oh, please, please understand. I will never get away with murder, not free and clear. My conscience won't let me."

Broken hearts and those who break them never get away with a thing. Weep for them both. I have no way of paying my debt. Not in this lifetime. In this lifetime, I'll punish myself every day with the harshest sentence of all, that of walking free.

All right, I know you're on to me now, that those last sentiments are over the top. My new life is not entirely devoid of mercy and absolution, not totally. I've still got Hal. I don't deserve him, but I have him. And Raven and Constantia. And my old pal, Rennie, even though she now lives too far away to share hugs.

I have often wondered why so many blessings have plopped into my lap when I merit none. I asked Mrs. Lupio's opinion on the subject once, and she said God has unknowable reasons for the manner in which he allocates grace. She's right, of course. And so was T.S. Eliot when he penned: "For us, there is only the trying. The rest is not our business."

And God only knows...I do try.

43

As I put my story of heartache and violence to rest, I want to ask you a question about a college psych class I came close to failing during my sophomore year in college. The professor told us in his final lecture: A secret is no secret if known by more than one person, for under those conditions, it surely will not be kept.

Does this apply, do you think, to my own appalling secret? I speculate on this at times, yet not with anxiety. For each individual who knows my secret has a compelling reason to keep it. After all, it's their secret too.

Take Rennie, for example. She announced to Hal and me as she was packing to go back to Texas that she was ready to have children of her own, with the right man, of course, the one to whom she was married, and she hoped Hal would not be jealous. You have permission to chuckle at that last sentiment. Rennie seemed to think this a novel idea, having children with Clark, her own husband. And I guess it was...for a free spirit like Ren. I was thankful to hear of her new plan. I felt it would cinch every inclination on her part to keep a certain secret.

And then there's Hal. He would never tell due to his belief, incorrect though it may be, that he could work his way out of personal guilt by taking care of me and my children, a lifelong commitment leaving no room for jail time.

And, lastly, there's me. Since I was never able to find a single other person to go along with my idea of not keeping the secret (to include Detective Smythe), I finally gave up. Ironically, the career law officer's reason for staying quiet was the only reason that embodied any true nobility, that of making sure Raven and Constantia remained secure with their mother. And, yes, it has also been the fundamental motivation for the rest of us – Rennie, Hal, and me. How many times have we said the same words to each other over the years? For the sake of the children…

My psych professor was wrong to give me a D in his class, and more wrong in his theory on secrets. He would have realized his error if he had met the cast of characters holding mine under lock and key. Any one of them would risk life and limb to keep it.

I hated watching Rennie pack to go home. Yet there was no longer any reason for her to stay. She was never going to finish her college work. She did not want to. What she wanted was to spend her last few days in Charleston helping Hal and me finish ours. "I was born to manage nincompoops like the two of you," she said, "not for teaching art to a passel of snot-nosed kids back in Texas."

And manage us, she did. Rennie is the reason Hal and I both completed our work even if she did not complete her own…unless you want to call my and Hal's work hers. And as sad as I felt watching her prepare to leave, I was thankful she was glad to be going. "It's all about family now," she said. "This time next year I hope to have a set of twins of my own. You'd better be thinking about family, too, Arly. Don't you dare cut Giselle and Stuart's parents out of Raven and Constantia's lives. I want you to go to their houses every summer and invite them to yours every holiday. And Hal's parents too. Promise me that. And always, always stay in touch with Mr. Pinckney and Tycie and me."

"I promise," I said in stunned contemplation of yet more lifetime commitments. "Rennie," I added with grateful tears, "in your own cockeyed way you've made me understand the importance of family." And then together we intoned the familiar phrase...for the sake for the children.

At the airport, minutes before Rennie went through security to her gate, she arranged her farewell party of four – Hal, Raven, Constantia, and me – in the precise way she wanted to remember us. When she finished positioning us, I found myself standing bookend on the left, Raven next to me, Constantia next to her, and Hal bookend on the right. Rennie insisted we hold hands in our line-up and be silent and still so she could look at us. Which she did for a long moment. I thought she was going to cry, but she didn't, not full out. She nodded approval, then walked away with a showy backward wave over her shoulder, I guess to hide the few tears that did escape.

Our quirky little group that she was leaving behind watched her go and kept on watching after she was out of sight, probably hoping she would come back and tell us what to do next. Fifteen seconds or so passed before Hal and I broke rank and looked sideways at each other over Raven and Constantia's sweet heads. It was a look acknowledging the end of an era. Rennie was gone; we were on our own; and there was nothing left to do but confront our future the best way we could.

I won't put you through the details of how Hal and I navigated the following months and years…together of all things. Though a few particulars may be of interest: Hal cut his long hair and donated it to cancer patients going through chemo. He also bought a cheap wardrobe of mainstream clothing, earned a teaching credential of his own, and got a job in the art department of the flagship high school in Mount Pleasant. Good for Hal! As for me, I'm humbled to report I finally realized my costly dream of teaching in Raven and Constantia's school. I hope that doesn't give you pause every year when you meet your children's new teachers. They aren't all murd… Well, you know what they all are not. The truth is I've found the majority to be quite nice. Those are the ones I try to emulate. Another thing you may be gratified to learn is we left the beach as a family. Hal went along with my idea that bohemian life on a barrier island was getting a bit fringy for the sake of the children, too many wild parties ha-ha-ha. And I went along with his request that we get involved in church. Hal got a huge kick out of relating to me his childhood memories of growing up in a Christian environment, and look how great he turned out. A second ha-ha-ha. I have to say the church thing has been a deeper experience for me than I ever dreamed it would be. I'm still working on the vernacular…remorse, confession, mercy, repentance, forgiveness, transformation, the deity of Jesus, salvation by grace, justification, sanctification, and the immutable nature of God's Truth. Apparently, Rennie had been wrong when she declared truth overrated. By the time I get the hang of it all, Raven and Constantia will be ready to be baptized. Hal wants the pastor to immerse the three of us on the same day in the same service, preferably in the Atlantic Ocean. He won't have to join us. He was baptized at age twelve, which meant his main priority after backsliding so badly was to get himself to an altar as soon as possible, rededicate his life to God, and reaffirm his belief that Jesus is God's Son who gave his life to save repentant sinners. Which is what sweet Hal did the very first Sunday we attended church in Mount Pleasant. I'm still learning about all these Spiritual concepts, so please don't judge me harshly. I love the people in our church, and if I ever make it to heaven, I'm sure I'll squeak through the pearly gates hanging onto their coattails. Every time I see Miss Jane Pringle, my favorite congregate (age 99), she assures me the concepts I'm trying to wrap my mind around are simpler than my brain wants to make them. I can't help but smile when she holds her chin high and belts out the first phrase of Edward Mote's old hymn: My hope is built on nothing less than Jesus' blood and righteousness." I love that it rhymes. I love that God saves us by His grace and the blood of His Son. And, because of the dear testimony of Miss Pringle's own servant-life, I love Jesus!"

After we left the beach cottage for good (though Raven and Constantia – and another little somebody I'll tell you about later – remained citizens of the Kingdom of Lupio), we moved into a modest house in a modest neighborhood off Highway 17, the old highway to Awendaw and Georgetown, where every single day we hope and pray with all our hearts that our diligent striving for the sake of the children will have a better chance of paying off. Don't laugh at us for aspiring to the middle class and not the upper.

Congratulate us. For we have discerned that the middle is the safest place for regular folks to reside. We purchased our home, albeit with the help of a fast-talking mortgage loan officer at a local bank, a big clue it had nothing to do with the Peregrine estate. Strike one for adult responsibility and paying one's own way. Not that Rennie or Stuart would buy into such a lame road to independence, a third ha-ha-ha.

And, finally, be happy to learn that my dear old best friend, Rennie, eventually gave birth to her own children. Two boys. Not twins, though. Fourteen months apart. The older one she named Hal and the younger one Sullivan. To this day, Clark, her loving husband, has no clue to the reason behind either name. That is part of the vaulted secret. And, to our everlasting joy, Hal and I had another baby girl, the other little somebody I mentioned earlier. We named her Reynolds, of course, after you-know-who. It is my fondest hope Baby Rennie will grow up to have a personality like her namesake. I surely don't want her to be like me. Everyone knows that somber ages faster than happy-go-lucky. And who likes somber anyway ? No one!

Oh, I almost forgot. Rennie left Betsy Ross (or a series of fishes just like her from the pet store whenever nature calls each current one home to glory) in the care of Raven and Constantia and now Baby Rennie. Betsy lives in the same goldfish bowl she has always occupied despite being loved to death (sometimes literally) with over-feeding. And no one swears on her life anymore. The newly reformed Hal forbids it. He has grown out of his silence and immaturity, though he did hang onto his ancient boom box on which he now plays praise songs. He also talks a great deal more, a good thing for Raven and Constantia and Baby Rennie, because their mother (me) still talks very little. Hal has been different to live with than Stuart ever was. He will answer any and all of my burning questions. I was grateful for how quickly he dispensed with the two biggest issues in my heart, those relative to his short and toxic relationship with Stuart. One: how did he get mixed up with Stuart in the first place? And two: Why in the name of heaven did Stuart give him a gun and what did he expect him to do with it? Unlike Stu, who would obfuscate about whether it was going to rain no matter if sheets of H2O were pouring down on his head, Hal routinely cut straight to the truth. How did he first meet Stuart? Simple. He answered an ad in the newspaper. Temporary part-time work for a college student in need of extra cash. Excellent pay. Call so-and-so. That was it. Hal called Stuart's cell, and the rest flowed from there. As for the gun, to my confusion, Hal swore up and down Stuart had nothing to do with it. To his knowledge, Stu never even knew it existed. It was Giselle who had given him the gun and bullets – all behind Stuart's back – on one of their last visits to Charleston. Chilling, huh. She told him it was for his own safety and security. Safety and security against what, Hal never knew and never asked. He just hid the gun and bullets in his new footlocker downstairs in the storeroom and kept on collecting greenbacks from Stuart without saying a word. I still feel sick when I think of Giselle and the gun. And me and the gun. And the two of us together and that horrible gun. I don't know what happened to it in the end, but guessing, I'd say it is in the possession of a certain retired homicide detective in Florida.

That about wraps things up, I suppose, although I do want to remind you of one hopeful thing I mentioned at the start, mainly because some of you might want to know if Hal and I ever tied the knot officially. I'll leave it to you to answer that question however your heart sees fit. Perhaps it would soothe your soul to answer it within the context of what I told you when I first introduced my story: I did not fall in love with Hal those first days. I trained myself to look away. He belonged to my friend, Rennie, a circumstance that made him off limits to me. Truth? Hal was too young for either one of us…too good-looking, distant, aimless, seductive, the sum of which rendered him irresistible to a free spirit like Rennie, who for a time was giving her wedding band a rest in its original Tiffany's box. I had no inconvenient husband lurking in the background just then, a fact that did not make me younger. It made me divorced. But we were talking about Hal, weren't we? Yes, about Hal. We were talking about him.

As time dragged by after the shooting – I killed my ex-husband's wife, you see, when she tried to steal my children – I discovered a certain sensitivity in Hal hiding beneath the surface, an unexpected warmth that on difficult days had the capacity to melt my frozen heart…around its icy edges at least. Though I still did not fall in love with him. That complication came later over the weeks it took him, along with Rennie, to show me in the context of the unspeakable what real love was all about. Forsake me, they did not. Love me, they did.

Thank you, God, for love. Amen.

The End

ABOUT THE AUTHOR

TERRY WARD TUCKER, PhD, is a graduate of the University of North Carolina at Chapel Hill. *Arlena Returns* is the sequel to her best-selling novel, *Charleston's Elegant Sinners.* Tucker's earlier novel, *Moonlight and Mill Whistles,* received *ForeWord Magazine*'s Silver Book of the Year Award. Winston Groom, author of *Forrest Gump* wrote, “Terry Ward Tucker tells a lovely and captivating story in *Moonlight and Mill Whistles.* Her writing is a joy to read.” Pat Conroy praised Tucker's lowcountry novel, *Moonbow Over Charleston.* “Terry Ward Tucker paints a moonbow upon Charleston’s night sky and gifts us all with its loveliness. Thank you, Terry!” Tucker also writes faith-based novels, screenplays, devotional books, and Bible discovery guides. Linda Flannery, Executive Producer, Inspire You Entertainment, wrote about Tucker's faith-based novel, *Moon River,* "Be inspired as Terry Ward Tucker draws you into the story of Anne York's battle with infertility. You'll find yourself, along with Anne, praying God-centered rather than self-centered prayers. Get a blessing! Read this book!" Terry served as screenplay co-writer for *Only God Can,* faith-based feature film produced by Inspire You Entertainment, and sole screenplay writer for *Hate Won’t Win,* a new movie in development based on the shooting massacre at Mother Emanuel Church in Charleston.

Made in the USA
Monee, IL
16 October 2024

67981258R00128